If I had been a son, I could have gone to fight in my father's place.

My father could have remained home and our family could still have kept its honor. But I was not a boy; I was a girl. A girl who could ride a horse, with or without a saddle. A girl who could shoot an arrow from a bow made for a tall, strong man and still hit her target. A girl who had never wanted what other girls want. A girl unlike any other girl in China.

I must not let my father go to fight, I thought. *I will not.*

I would not watch my father ride away, and then stay behind to comfort my stepmother as she cried herself to sleep at night. I loved them both too much. And I had waited too long for my father to come home in the first place to stand in the door of our home now and watch him ride away to die.

And so I would do the only thing I could to protect both my father's life and our family's honor: I would go to fight in his place. I would prove myself to be my father's child, even if I was a daughter.

Once upon a Time

WILD ORCHID

A Retelling of "The Ballad of Mulan"

BY CAMERON DOKEY

SIMON PULSE

New York   London   Toronto   Sydney

SIMON PULSE

An imprint of Simon & Schuster Children's Publishing Division

1230 Avenue of the Americas, New York, NY 10020

Copyright © 2009 by Cameron Dokey

All rights reserved, including the right of

reproduction in whole or in part in any form.

SIMON PULSE and colophon are registered trademarks

of Simon & Schuster, Inc.

The text of this book was set in Adobe Jenson.

Manufactured in the United States of America

First Simon Pulse paperback edition February 2009

2 4 6 8 10 9 7 5 3

Library of Congress Control Number 2008932845

ISBN-13: 978-1-4169-7168-9

ISBN-10: 1-4169-7168-8

*For Suzanne, Rosa, Anne, Sara, and Michel,
the gang at Cameron Catering without
whose support Mulan's adventures would
not have been possible*

ONE

When the wild wood orchids bloom in the spring, pushing their brave faces from beneath the fallen leaves of winter, that is when mothers like to take their daughters on their knees and sing to them "The Ballad of Mulan," the story of the girl who saved all of China. For if you listen closely to the syllables of that name, this is what you'll hear there: *mu*—"wood"; *lan*—"orchid."

Listening is a good habit to learn for its own sake, as is the art of looking closely. All of us show many faces to the world. No one shows her true face all the time. To do that would be dangerous, for what is seen can also be known. And what is known can be out-maneuvered, outguessed. Lifted up, or hunted down. Uncovering that which is hidden is a fine and delicate skill, as great a weapon for a warrior to possess as a bow or a sword.

I sound very wise and knowledgeable for someone not yet twenty, don't I?

I certainly didn't sound that way at the beginning of my adventure. And there are plenty of times even now when wise and knowledgeable is not the way I sound, or feel. So what do I feel? A reasonable question, which deserves an honest answer.

I feel . . . fortunate.

I have not led an ordinary life, nor a life that would suit everyone. I took great risks, but because I did, I also earned great rewards. I found the way to show my true face freely, without fear. Because of this, I found true love.

Oh, yes. And I did save China.

But I am getting very far ahead of myself.

I was born in the year of the monkey, and I showed the monkey's quick and agile mind from the start, or so Min Xian, my nanny, always told me. I shared the monkey's delight in solving puzzles, its ability to improvise. Generally this took the form of escaping from places where I was supposed to stay put, and getting into places I wasn't supposed to go. My growing up was definitely a series of adventures, followed by bumps, bruises, and many scoldings.

There was the time I climbed the largest plum tree on our grounds, for instance. When the plum trees were in bloom, you could smell their sweetness from a distance so great I never could figure out quite how far it was. One year, the year I turned seven, I set myself a goal: to watch the highest bud on the tallest tree become a blossom. The tallest tree was my favorite. Ancient and gnarled, it stood with its feet in a stream that marked the boundary between my family's property and that of my closet friend—my only friend, in fact—a boy named Li Po.

Seven is considered an important age in China. In our seventh year, childhood comes to an end. Girls begin the lessons that will one day make them proper young women, and boys begin the lessons that will make them proper young men.

Li Po was several months older than me. He had already begun the first of his lessons, learning to read and write. My own would be much less interesting— as far as I was concerned, anyway. I would be taught to weave, to sew, and to embroider. Worst of all was the fact that all these lessons would occur in the very last place I wanted to be: indoors.

So in a gesture of defiance, on the morning of my seventh birthday, I woke up early, determined to climb the ancient plum tree and not come down until the bud I had my eye on blossomed. You can probably guess what happened next. I climbed higher than I should have, into branches that would not hold my weight, and, as a result, I fell. Old Lao, who looked after any part of the Hua family compound that Min Xian did not, claimed it was a wonder I didn't break any bones. I had plummeted from the top of the tree to the bottom, with only the freshly turned earth of the orchard to break my fall. The second wonder was that I hit the ground at all, and did not fall into the stream, which was shallow and full of stones.

Broken bones I may have been spared, but I still hit the earth with enough force to knock even the *thought* of breath right out of my lungs. For many moments all I could do was lie on my back, waiting for my breath to return, and gaze up through the dark branches of the tree at the blue spring sky beyond. And in this way I saw the first bud unfurl. So I suppose you could say that I accomplished what I'd set out to, after all.

Another child might have decided it was better, or at least just as good, to keep her feet firmly on the ground from then on. Had I not accomplished what I'd wanted? Could I not have done so standing beneath the tree and gazing upward, thereby saving myself the pain and trouble of a fall?

I, of course, derived another lesson entirely: I should practice climbing more.

This I did, escaping from my endless lessons whenever I could to climb any vertical surface I could get my unladylike hands on. I learned to climb, and to cling, like a monkey, living up to the first promise of my horoscope, and I never fell again, save once. The exception is a story in and of itself, which I will tell you in its own good time.

But in my determination not to let gravity defeat me I revealed more than just a monkey's heart. For it is not only the animal of the year of our births that helps to shape who we are. There are also the months and the hours of our births to consider. These contribute animals, and attributes, to our personalities as well. It's important to pay attention to these creatures because, if you watch them closely, you will discover that they are the ones who best reveal who we truly are.

I was born in the month of the dog.

From the dog I derive these qualities: I am a seeker of justice, honest and loyal. But I am also persistent, willing to perform a task over and over until I get it right. I am, in other words, *dogged*. Once I've set my heart on something, there's no use trying to convince me to give it up—and certainly not without a fight.

But there is still one animal more. The creature I am in my innermost heart of hearts, the one who claimed me for its own in the hour in which I was born. This is my secret animal, the most important one of all.

If the traits I acquired in the year of my birth are the flesh, and the month of my birth are the sinews of who I am, then the traits that became mine at the hour of my birth are my spine, my backbone. More difficult to see but forming the structure on which all the rest depends.

And in my spine, at the very core of me, I am a tiger. Passionate and daring, impetuous, longing to rebel. Unpredictable and quick-tempered. But also determined and as obstinate as a solid wall of *shidan*—stone.

Min Xian, who even in her old age possessed the best eyesight of anyone I ever knew, claims she saw and understood these things about me from the first moment she saw me, from the first time she heard me cry. Never had she heard a baby shriek so loudly, or so she claimed, particularly not a girl.

It was as if I were announcing that I was going to

be different right from the start. This was only fitting, Min Xian said, for different is precisely what I was. Different from even before I drew that first breath; different from the moment I had been conceived. Different in my very blood, a direct bequest from both my parents. It was this that made my uniqueness so strong.

I had to take Min Xian's word for all of this, for I did not know my parents when I was growing up. My father was the great soldier Hua Wei. Throughout my childhood, and for many years before that, my father fought bravely in China's cause. Though it would be many years before I saw him face-to-face, I heard tales of my father's courage, discipline, and bravery from the moment my ears first were taught to listen.

My mother's name I never heard at all, just as I never saw her face nor heard her voice, for she died the day that I was born.

But the tale of how my parents came to marry I did hear. It was famous, repeated not just in our household but throughout all China. In a time when marriages were carefully arranged for the sake of family honor and social standing, when a bride and groom might meet in the morning and be married that same afternoon, my parents had done the unthinkable.

They had married for love.

It was all the emperor's doing, of course. Without the blessing of the Son of Heaven, my parents' union would never have been possible. My father, Hua Wei, was a soldier, as I have said. He had fought and won many battles for China's cause. In the years before I was born and for many years thereafter, our northern borders were often under attack by a fierce, proud people whom we called the Huns. There were many in our land who also called them barbarians. My father was not among them.

"You must never call your enemy by a name you choose for him, Mulan," he told me when we finally met, when I was all but grown. "Instead you must call him by the name he calls himself. What he chooses will reflect his pride; it will reveal his desires. But what you choose to call him will reveal your fears, which should be kept to yourself, lest your enemy find the way to exploit them."

There was a reason he had been so successful against the Huns, according to my father. Actually, there was more than one: My father never underestimated them, and he recognized that, as foreign as they seemed, they were also men, just as he was a man. Capable of coveting what other men possessed. Willing to fight to claim it for themselves. And what the Huns desired most, or so it seemed, was China.

To this end, one day more than a year before I was born, the Son of Heaven's best-loved son was snatched away by a Hun raiding party. My father rescued him and returned him to the safety of his father's arms. In gratitude the Son of Heaven promoted Hua Wei to general. But he did not stop there. He also granted my father an astonishing reward.

"You have given me back the child who holds the first place in my heart," the emperor told my father. "In return, I will grant the first wish your heart holds."

My father was already on his knees, but at the Son of Heaven's words he bowed even lower, and pressed his forehead to the ground. Not only was this the fitting way to show his thanks, it was also the perfect way for my father to cover his astonishment and give himself time to think. The boy that he had rescued, Prince Jian, was not yet ten years old and was not the emperor's only son. There were two older boys who might, as time went on, grow to become jealous of the fact that their younger brother held the greatest share of the Son of Heaven's heart.

At this prince's birth the soothsayers had proclaimed many omens, none of them understood in their entirety, for that is the way of such prophecies. One thing, however, seemed as clear as glass: It was Prince Jian's destiny to help determine the fate of China.

"My heart has what it desires, Majesty," my father finally said. "For it wants nothing more than to serve you."

It was a safe and diplomatic answer, at which it is said that the Son of Heaven smiled.

"You are doing that already," he replied. "And I hope you will continue to do so for many years to come. But listen to me closely: I command you now to choose one thing more. Do so quickly or you will make me angry. And do not speak with a courtier's tongue. I would have your heart speak—it is strong, and you have shown me that it can be trusted."

"As the Son of Heaven commands, so I shall obey," my father promised.

"Excellent," the emperor said. "Now let me see your face."

And so, though he remained on his knees, my father looked into the Son of Heaven's face when he spoke the first wish of his heart.

"It is long past time for me to marry," Hua Wei said. "If it pleases you, I ask that I be allowed to choose my own bride. Long has my heart known the lady it desires, for we grew up together. I have given the strength of my mind and body to your service gladly, but now let my heart serve itself. Let it choose love."

The Son of Heaven was greatly moved by my father's words, as were all who stood within earshot. The emperor agreed to my father's request at once. He gave him permission to return to his home in the countryside. My parents were married before the week was out. They then spent several happy months together, far away from the bustle of the court and the city, in the house where my father had grown up. But all the time the threat of war hung over their happiness. In the autumn my father was called back to the emperor's service to fight the Huns once more.

My father knew a baby was on the way when he departed. Of course, both my parents hoped that I would be a boy. I cannot fault them for this. Their thinking on the subject was no different from anyone else's. It is a son who carries on the family name, who cares for his parents when they grow old. Girls are gifts to be given in marriage to other families, to provide *them* with sons.

My young mother went into labor while her beloved husband was far away from home. If he had stayed by her side, might she have lived? Might she have proved strong enough to bring me into the world and still survive? There's not much point in asking such questions. I know this, but even so . . . I cannot help but wonder, sometimes, what my life would have been like if my mother had lived. Would I have learned to be more like other girls, or would the parts of me that made me so different still have made their presence felt?

If my mother had lived, might my father have come home sooner? Did he delay his return, not wishing to see the child who had taken away his only love, the first wish of his innermost heart?

When word reached him of my mother's death, it is said my father's strong heart cracked clean in two, and that the sound could be heard for miles around, even over the noise of war. For the one and only time in his life, the great general Hua Wei wept. And from that moment forward he forbade anyone to speak my mother's name aloud. The very syllables of her name were like fresh wounds, further scarring his already maimed and broken heart.

My mother had loved the tiny orchids that grow in the woods near our home. Those flowers are the true definition of "wild"—not just unwilling but *unable* to be tamed. A tidy garden bed, careful tending and watering—these things do not suit them at all. They cannot be transplanted. They must be as they are, or not at all.

With tears streaming down his cheeks my father named me for those wild plants—those *yesheng zhiwu*, wild wood orchids. In so doing he helped to set my feet upon a path unlike that of any other girl in China.

Even in his grief my father named me well, for the name he gave me was *Mulan*.

Two

My father might have left the "wild" out of my name, but it made no difference. It was still there inside me, running with the very blood in my veins, the blood that made me different from any other girl in China.

Min Xian did her best to tame me. Or, failing that, to render me not so wild as to bring the family dishonor. She had raised my mother before me, so she knew her business, and my father was bound to return someday, after all.

"You don't know that," I said crossly one night after a particularly stern scolding. Many years had passed since my fall out of the plum tree. I had just celebrated my thirteenth birthday. I was almost a young woman now. I would soon be old enough to become a bride. Whether I was wiser was a point Min Xian was always more than happy to debate, and I have to admit that the events of this particular day only served to prove her point.

I was covered from head to toe with bruises. As his birthday gift my best friend, Li Po, had offered to teach me how to use a sword.

The march toward adulthood had done nothing to diminish our friendship. If anything, it had only made us closer. Teaching me swordplay was just the latest in a long line of lessons Li Po had provided, which included learning to read and write, to shoot a bow and arrow, and to ride a horse.

The sword he'd offered to teach me with that day was only made of wood. We could not have truly injured each other. But a wooden sword can raise as fine and painful a welt as you are likely to see or feel, let me tell you.

I might have kept my sword lessons, and my bruises, a secret were it not for the fact that Min Xian still insisted on giving me my baths from time to time. In vain had I protested that at thirteen I was old enough and competent enough to bathe myself.

"I cared for your mother until the day she died," Min Xian declared stoutly. She made a flapping motion with her arms, as if shooing geese, to encourage me to move on along to the bathhouse. "What was good enough for her will be good enough for you, my fine young lady."

I opened my mouth to protest but then closed it again. Her voice might have sounded stern, but I knew from experience that Min Xian called me "young lady" only when she was upset about something. It didn't take much to figure out what it was.

Though she obeyed my father's orders, it had always bothered Min Xian that she could not speak my mother's name aloud to me, my mother's only child. In particular it pained her because she knew that learning my mother's name was the first of the three great wishes of my heart.

The other two things I wished for were that my father would discover that he loved me after all and that he would then come home. Neither of these last wishes was within Min Xian's power to grant, of course. This sometimes made her grouchy, around my birthday in particular. The day of one's birth is a time for the granting of wishes, not withholding them. And so I let her herd me toward the bathhouse, saving my voice for the explanations I knew I would soon be making.

When Min Xian saw my bruises, she hissed in sympathy and outrage combined.

"What on earth did you do to acquire those?" she asked, and then raised a bony hand. "On second thought, don't tell me. I want to be able to answer with a clean heart when Li Po's mother shows up, demanding if I know what you've been up to with her son."

"She isn't going to do that, and you know it," I answered. I sank into the fragrant bathwater, hissing myself as the hot water found my bruises one by one.

Li Po's mother fancied herself a great lady, and she did not care for my friendship with her son. The only thing that kept her from forbidding it altogether was the Hua family name, older and more respected than her own.

In particular Li Po's mother feared Li Po and I might follow in my parents' footsteps and fall in love. If Li Po asked for my hand and my father consented to the match, then his mother would have to accept me as her daughter-in-law whether she liked it or not. Ours was the older, more respected family. Marrying me would be a step up in the world for Li Po.

The fact that neither Li Po nor I had ever expressed the slightest wish to marry made no difference to his mother. Her son was young and handsome. The two of us had grown up together. Why should the day not come when we would fall in love? But Li Po's mother believed, as most people did, that love before marriage was not to be desired. It was unnatural; it complicated more things than it solved.

I wondered how Li Po's family would feel if they knew about the lessons he gave me, which were every bit as radical as marrying for love.

I'd never been able to figure out quite how Li Po managed to sneak away to give me the lessons he did, but I think it was because his family was more traditional than mine. Where I had only Min Xian and Old Lao, Li Po was surrounded by family, by aunts, uncles, and cousins, all forming one great and complex web where every member of the family knew precisely who they were in relation to everyone else.

It was both binding and liberating because with so many people around, it was easy for Li Po to slip away from time to time. By the time knowledge of his absence made its way through the family channels,

Li Po was back where he belonged. This was the way most families operated. It was mine that fell outside the norm.

Yet another aspect of my parents' relationship that made them unusual was that each had been an only child. I had no cousins to run with, no aunties to help raise me, no uncles to help manage my father's estate while he was away fighting the Huns. I had only servants. The fact that I loved them as family made no difference. We were not true family, not related by blood. Save for my father, I had no one.

"Li Po's teaching me how to use a sword," I told Min Xian.

"Stop! Enough!" she cried as she began to scrub my back vigorously enough to bring tears to my eyes. "I told you, I do not wish to know."

"You do too," I countered, though my teeth threatened to rattle with the scrubbing. "Otherwise, how will you fuss?"

Quick as lightning, Min Xian gave me a dunk. I came up sputtering, wiping water from my eyes.

"First reading and writing, then archery and riding, and now this," she went on before I could so much as take a breath to protest, or get a word in edgewise. "What your father will say when he comes home I cannot imagine."

"You don't have to," I gasped out, as I finally managed to wriggle free and scoot out of the reach of Min Xian's strong arm. I dunked my own head this time, tossing my hair back as I surfaced.

16

"We both know he'll say nothing at all. My father hasn't come home once, not in thirteen years. What makes you think he'll ever come home? If he wanted to see me, he'd have come back long ago."

Min Xian gazed at me, her lips pursed, as if she tasted something bitter that she longed to spit out.

"Your father serves the emperor," she said finally. "He has a place, a duty to perform." She frowned at me, just in case I was missing the point of her words, which, for the record, I was not.

"As do we all," she finished up.

"He'd have come home if I were a boy," I said sullenly. "Or sent word for me to go to him."

He'd have found a way to love me in spite of his sorrow over my mother's death, if I had been a son.

"You can't know what someone else will do ahead of time," Min Xian pronounced.

"That's not what Li Po says," I countered. "He says his tutor tells him that a man's actions can be predicted. That you can know what he *will* do by what he has, and has not, already done."

"That sounds like a lot of scholarly nonsense, if you ask me," Min Xian snorted. "You can never know everything about a person, for we each carry at least one secret."

"And what secret is that?" I inquired, intrigued now, in spite of myself.

"What we hold deep inside our hearts," Min Xian replied. "Until we release it, no mind can fathom what we will do. Sometimes not even our own."

She made an impatient gesture, as if to show she had had enough philosophizing. "The water's turning cold," she said. "Rinse the rest of that soap out of your hair. Then come sit by the fire so it can dry."

For once I did as Min Xian wished without argument, as she was right. The water did feel cold. But more than that, I obeyed her because she'd also given me something to think about.

Was there a secret hiding in my father's broken heart? If so, what was it? Maybe if I could discover what it was, I could finally find the way to make him love me.

THREE

Sitting on a low stool before the fire, I thought all evening about what Min Xian had said, my hair fanned out across my shoulders and back as I waited for it to dry. Usually drying my hair drives me crazy. I have to sit still for far too long. My hair is long and thick. It flows down my back like a river of ink. Waiting for it to dry seems to take forever. That night, however, I was content to sit still and think.

What secrets did the hearts around me hold? What secrets did mine hold? Now that I was taking the time to stop and consider, I could see that it was not Li Po's clever young tutor who understood people best. It was old Min Xian.

All of us hold something unexpected deep within ourselves. Something even we may not suspect or recognize. While our heart's rhythm may seem steady, so steady that we take it for granted, this does not mean the heart is not also full of wonders and surprises. That it beats in the first place may be the most surprisingly wonderful thing of all.

Without warning I felt my lips curve into a smile as one of the great surprises of my life popped into my mind, the day Li Po had first offered to share his lessons with me.

"I know you're up there, so you might as well come down," he'd called.

It was several weeks after that fateful seventh birthday. I was back in the plum tree, of course. Though I was trying my best to master my new assignments, wishing to make my father proud of me even from afar, the bald truth was that I found them boring.

If I had lived in the city, in Chang'an, my family's high status would have meant that I might at least be taught to read and write. But I did not live in the capital. I lived in the country, and neither Min Xian nor Old Lao could teach me such skills, for they did not know how. My father might have arranged a tutor for me, to remedy the situation, but he did not. On this as on every other aspect of my upbringing he remained silent. I tried to tell myself I did not mind this neglect.

I have never been very good at lying, not even to myself.

And so I was left to learning the tasks that Min Xian thought appropriate and could teach me. Of my three main assignments—sewing, weaving, and embroidery—I disliked embroidery the most. I simply could not see the purpose of learning all those fine stitches, particularly as I wore plain clothes.

Most days I wore a long, straight tunic over a countrywoman's pants, and sturdy shoes that were good for being outdoors. My closet contained no embroidered slippers with curled toes, no brightly colored silk dresses with long, flowing sleeves and plunging necklines. Nor did I wear hairstyles so elaborate they could only be held in place by jeweled or enameled combs—hairstyles bearing names such as *yunji*, "resembling clouds," or *hudie ji*, "resembling the wings of a butterfly."

Instead I wore my hair in a long braid that fell straight down the center of my back. Most of the time I looked like a simple country girl, except for the days when I tucked my braid down the back of my tunic to keep it from getting caught on whatever tree I was climbing. On those days I looked like a boy. At no time did I look like the child of one of the greatest generals in all of China.

So when the day came that my embroidery needle would not cooperate no matter how carefully I tried to ply it—and the needle thrust deeply into one of my fingers, drawing bright drops of blood—I threw both the fabric on which I was working and the needle to the floor in disgust. What difference did it make that I was trying hard to learn my lessons? Trying to make my absent father proud? He was never going to see a single one of my accomplishments, even if I mastered them to perfection.

He was never going to see me, because I was just a girl, and my father, the great general Hua Wei, was never coming home.

Leaving my embroidery in a heap on the floor, I

left the house. As always I headed for the ancient plum tree. It was where I always went when my emotions ran high, both in good times and in bad. And it was there that Li Po found me, for he knew just where to look.

"I can see you, you know. So you might as well come down."

"You can't either. I'm invisible," I said. "Now go away and leave me alone."

Another person might have taken me at my word, but Li Po did not. Instead he took a seat beneath the tree on a broad, flat rock that rested beside the stream. This was a favorite place, as well. Peering down through the branches, I could see Li Po had a long stick in one hand. He leaned over and began to make markings in the soft, damp earth beside the rock.

"I can stay here if I want to," he finally replied. "I'm on my family's side of the stream."

This was true enough, a fact that made me only more annoyed. I was in a mood to argue, not to be reasonable, and certainly not to give in. And my finger hurt, besides.

"Tell me what you're doing, then," I called down.

"Why should I?" asked Li Po. He continued moving the stick. "You're invisible, and a grouch."

"Try spending your day embroidering birds and flowers and see how you like it," I said.

Li Po stopped what he was doing and looked up.

"Embroidery again? I'm sorry, Mulan."

"Yes, well, you should be," I said, though even as I made my pronouncement, I knew Li Po was trying to make me feel better. The fact that he got to learn to read and write while I had to learn embroidery stitches was not his fault. And suddenly I knew what he'd been doing with the stick.

"You're writing—drawing characters—aren't you?" I asked. "Will you show me how?"

"I will if you come down," Li Po replied. "You'll give me a crick in the neck otherwise, trying to look up at you."

I climbed down. As I'd been practicing this a lot, it didn't take me very long. Soon I had crossed the stream and was kneeling on the rock beside Li Po, gazing down at the images he'd etched in the mud. I pointed to the closest one.

"That looks like a man," I said.

"It does, doesn't it?" Li Po nodded. "What do you think it represents?"

I narrowed my eyes, as if this might help me decipher the character's meaning. It couldn't simply be "*man.*" That was too obvious.

"Is it a particular kind of man?" I asked. "A soldier?"

"No," Li Po said. "But you're thinking along the right lines. Think of something a soldier must have.

Not something extra, like a shield or sword, but . . ." He paused, as if searching for the right term. "An attribute. Something inside himself. Something you can figure out just by looking at the character."

Totally engrossed now, I gazed down at what Li Po had created. It really *did* look like a soldier, a helmet on his head, one arm extending out in front, as if to protect his body from a blow. The other hand rested on his hip, as if on the hilt of his sword. Just below it the back leg seemed bent, as if to carry all the weight. The front leg was fully extended, giving the whole figure an air of alertness, ready to pounce at a moment's notice.

But try as I might I couldn't quite make the connection between the form and what it represented.

"Determination?" I hazarded a guess.

"Close," Li Po said. He gave me a sidelong glance, as if to judge my temper. "Do you want me to tell you, or do you want to keep on guessing?"

"Tell me," I said at once. I wanted to understand more than I wanted to say I'd figured it out myself.

"Courage," Li Po declared, at which I clapped my hands.

"Of course!" I cried. "He's not certain what is coming next, so he holds one arm in front to protect himself, but he's also ready to attack if he needs to. Uncertain but prepared. Courageous."

I gazed at the character, as new possibilities seemed to explode inside my head.

"Does it always make you feel like this?" I asked.

"Like what?"

By way of an answer I captured Li Po's hand, pressing his fingers against the inside of my wrist. You could feel my heart beat there, hard and fast, as if I'd just run a race.

Li Po gave a sudden grin, understanding at once. "Yes," he said. "Every time I grasp a new meaning, it feels just like that."

"Can you show me how to draw the character?"

Li Po placed the stick in my hand and then closed his fingers over mine. "You begin this way," he said.

Together we made the stroke that ran straight up and down. That seemed to me to be the soldier's backbone. The rest followed from there. Within a few moments we had reproduced the character together. Li Po took his hand away.

"Now you try it on your own."

It was harder than it looked. I performed the motions half a dozen more times before re-creating the character to both Li Po's satisfaction and my own. I sat back on my heels, the stick still clutched in my fist, gazing at the row of tiny soldiers marching across the earth in front of me.

"It's beautiful," I said. "Much more beautiful than embroidery."

"It wouldn't look as nice on a dress," Li Po commented.

I laughed, too pleased and exhilarated to let his teasing make a dent in my joy.

"I don't care," I said. "I don't own any fancy dresses anyhow."

I poked the tip of the stick into the wet earth, a frown snaking down between my brows.

"What?" Li Po asked.

I jabbed a little harder. "Nothing," I said, which was a big, fat lie. But I wasn't sure how to ask for what I wanted. *Courage, Mulan*, I suddenly thought.

"Willyouteachme?" I asked, the words coming out so quickly it sounded as if they were one. I took a breath and then tried again. "The characters you're learning, will you teach me more of them? I know my father hasn't said I may, but I want to study them so much and I . . ."

All of a sudden I felt light-headed, and so I drew in a breath. "I think it's what my mother would have wanted."

Li Po was silent for a moment. "It must be awful," he finally said. "Not even knowing what she was called."

Without warning Li Po sat up straight, as if he'd been the one poked with my embroidery needle. "I know," he exclaimed. "We could make up a name, a secret name, one we'd never tell anyone. That way you'd have something to call her. You'd be able to talk to her, if you wanted to."

He squirmed a little on the hard rock seat, as if he'd grown uncomfortable. But I knew that wasn't it at all. Li Po was excited, just as I was.

"If I choose, will you show me how to write it?"

"I will," Li Po promised. "Pretend you're about to make a wish. Close your eyes. Then open them and tell me what you want your mother's name to be."

I inhaled deeply, closing my eyes. I listened to the water in the stream. I felt the warmth of the late afternoon sun beating down. And the name popped into my head, almost as if it had been waiting there all along.

"*Zao Xing*," I said as I opened my eyes. "Morning Star."

"That's beautiful," Li Po said. "And look, the characters that form it look almost the same." Quickly he drew them, side by side.

"Thank you," I breathed when he was finished. Never had I been given a more wonderful gift. "Thank you, Li Po."

He smiled. "You're welcome, Little Orchid."

I made a rude sound. "I'm big enough to dump you in the stream," I threatened.

"Yes, but if you do that, I won't teach you how to read and write," Li Po replied.

I threw my arms around him. "You'll teach me? Honestly? You'll teach me everything you learn yourself?"

"Everything I learn myself," Li Po promised. "Now and forever. You're my best friend. I love you, Mulan."

"And I love you," I said. I kept my arms around him tight. "Let's make a pact," I said fiercely. "No matter what happens, let's promise to be friends for life."

"Friends for life," Li Po echoed as he returned

my hug. "But we'll have to be careful, Mulan. You have to work hard at your own lessons too. If my family finds out what we're doing, they'll split us up for good."

"I know. I'll be careful, and I'll work hard. Honestly I will," I vowed. "It's just . . . being a girl is so hard sometimes. It always seems to be about pleasing somebody else."

"Then you must master your lessons as best you can so that you can find the way to please yourself."

I released him and sat back, my hands on my hips. "What makes you so wise, all of a sudden?"

"I'm going to be a great scholar someday. Haven't you heard? Everybody says so."

"Everybody being your mother, you mean," I said. But I stood up and made a bow. "I am honored to become the first student of the great master Li Po."

"I'm going to remember that, to make sure you pay me the proper respect," Li Po said. And then he grinned. "Now sit back down. There's one more character I want to show you."

I settled back in beside him. Li Po leaned forward and drew a character comprised of just four lines.

The first was a downward swipe, slanting right to left. This was followed by a quick stroke across it to form a *T*, moving left to right.

Then on the right side of the down stroke, just beneath the place where the two lines crossed, Li Po made a line that started boldly toward the right. Before it went far, though, it abruptly changed direction, sweeping back to the left and down so that it looked like a man's leg bent at the knee.

Li Po lifted the stick and then put the tip to the earth and made one last stroke, left to right, angling down just beneath the bent leg.

Finally he lifted the stick and sat back, his eyes on me.

I studied the character. I was almost certain I knew what it meant, but I didn't want to rush into anything. I wanted to take my time making up my mind.

"Give me your hand," I said.

Li Po reached out and placed his palm on top of mine. We clasped hands, squeezing them together tightly, and I knew that I was right.

Just below that sudden bending of the knee was a space, a triangle. And it was in this space that the character's meaning resided. For this was its center, its true heart.

It's just four lines, I thought. But placed so cleverly together that they represent two entities, joining in such a way as to create something else. That secret triangle, as if formed by two hands clasped.

"It's *'friend,'* isn't it?" I said.

"That's it precisely," Li Po answered with a smile.

There was no more discussion after that. No more lessons, no more talk. Instead my only friend and I sat together, hands clasped tightly, until the light left the sky and we headed home.

FOUR

In the years that followed there were many lessons, and the pact of friendship Li Po and I had forged that day continued to grow strong. Every time Li Po learned something new from his tutors, he taught me to master it as well. It wasn't long before I had added riding and archery to my list of unladylike skills. And so over the years a curious event transpired, though I don't think either Li Po or I realized it at the time.

I stopped being quite so wild, at least on the inside.

While the new skills I was mastering were considered very masculine, they also took hard work, dedication, and time. In other words they took discipline, and not even I could be disciplined and wild all at the same time.

Acting with discipline requires you to know your true nature and, having come to know it, to bring it under control. On the surface I might have appeared unruly and unladylike, preferring boys' tasks to my own. But I kept the promise I had made the day of my first writing lesson. I learned my own tasks as well as the ones Li Po set for me. There wasn't a girl in all

China who had my unusual combination of skills, no matter that I looked like a simple country girl on the outside.

I still struggled at certain tasks, as if my hands were clumsy and unwilling to perform those skills that did not also fire my imagination or touch my heart. But Li Po had no such problem. It sometimes seemed to me that there was magic in Li Po's fingers, so deftly could he master anything he put his mind to.

Nowhere was this more apparent than when we practiced archery. I loved these lessons above all others, with the possible exception of horseback riding. When I rode, I could imagine I was free, imagine I was someplace where I didn't need to hide my own unusual accomplishments. A place that didn't require me to hide my own true face, but let me show it bravely and proudly. A place where I could be whomever I wanted.

In the absence of such a place, however, I practiced my archery.

I loved the feel of the bowstring against my fingers, pressing into my flesh, the stretch and burn of the muscles across my shoulders and back as I pulled the string back and held it taut. I loved the sensation in my legs as I planted them solidly against the earth, rooting me to it, making us one. It is not the air that gives the arrow its ability to fly. The air is full of currents, quick and mischievous, ready to send the arrow's flight off course. The thing that makes the arrow fly true is the ground. The ground calls to the arrow, making the arrow long to find its target and then return to earth, bringing its prize home.

I never lost my joy in setting the arrow free. Always it was as wonderful as it had been the very first time. I loved to watch it streaking toward the target, my heart not far behind it. On its way to the destination I intended and nowhere else.

On a good day, anyhow.

If I could have spent all my days shooting and retrieving arrows, I would have. But as good as I became, I could not match Li Po's skill. There were times when it seemed to me that he and the arrow shared some secret language, whispering together as Li Po held the feathers against his cheek, waiting patiently, watching his target, before letting the arrow fly. I could hit eight out of any ten targets we chose, but Li Po could hit anything at which he aimed, no matter how far away it was.

"Let me see you hit that," I challenged him late one summer afternoon. It was the time of day when we most often managed to snatch a few hours together. We were in our favorite place alongside the stream that separated his family's lands from mine. We often practiced shooting here, for there were many aspects to take into account—the steepness of the banks and the breath of the wind—and, of course, there were plenty of plums to use for targets.

The particular plum I had suggested as today's target was small, hanging on a branch toward the back of the tree. In order to pierce the target, Li Po would have to send his arrow through the heart of the tree, through many other branches filled with leaves and fruit.

I paced the bank opposite the tree. We were standing on Li Po's family's side of the stream.

"Shoot from here," I finally instructed. The place I selected was higher than the tree branch. Li Po would have to angle his shot down. This is always more difficult, because it's harder to judge the distance.

Li Po moved to stand beside me, eyeing both the branch and the location I had chosen, and then he gave a grunt. I stepped aside. Quickly Li Po took an arrow from the quiver on his back and set it to the bow. Then he set his feet in precisely the way that he had taught me, feeling the ground with his toes. Only when he was satisfied with his footing did he raise the bow and pull the arrow back, keeping his body relaxed even as the bowstring stretched taut.

For several seconds he stood just so. The wind moved the branches of the tree. I saw it ruffle the hair on Li Po's brow so that the hair threatened to tickle his eyes. He never even blinked. Then, for a moment, the wind fell away, and the instant that it ceased to breathe, Li Po let the arrow fly.

Straight across the stream it flew, passing amid the branches of the plum tree as if they weren't there at all. The arrow pierced the plum that was the target and then carried it to earth. I laughed and clapped my hands in appreciation as Li Po flashed a smile. Then, before I realized what he intended, Li Po bounded down the slope of the bank, splashed across the stream, and clambered up the opposite side to retrieve both his arrow and the plum.

He wiped the tip of the arrow on the grass and then thrust it back into his quiver. Returning to the stream, he bent to hold the plum in the cool water, washing the dirt from its pierced skin before straightening up and popping the small fruit into his mouth. He chewed vigorously, purple juice running down his chin. Then he spat the pit into the water and wiped a hand across his face. The grin he was wearing still remained, I noticed.

"I'll race you to the top of the tree," he challenged.

"No fair!" I cried. He had only to turn and take half a dozen steps to reach the tree's thick trunk. I was standing on the opposite bank. I still had the stream to cross.

I acted without thinking, just as Min Xian was always scolding me for doing. Taking several steps back to gather momentum before abruptly sprinting forward, I streaked toward the stream, my legs pumping as hard as they could go. As I ran, I gave what I fondly imagined was a fierce warrior's yell. I just had time to see Li Po's startled expression before I jumped.

Li Po's cry of warning came as I flew through the air, my arms stretched out in front. *Oh great dragon of the water,* I prayed as I flew across the stream. *Carry me safely above you. Help me reach my goal in safety. Or, if you cannot and I must fall, please don't let me break too many bones.*

No sooner had I finished my silent prayer than I sailed into the branches of the plum tree, hands and legs scrabbling for purchase but finding none. I slithered downward, leaves and plums showering around me, thin branches snapping against my face. Then, with a bone-jarring impact, my body finally found a branch that would hold it.

I wrapped my arms and legs around it, clinging like a monkey. I stayed that way for several moments, sucking air, feeling my heart knock against my ribs at my close call. When I had my breath back, I decided it was time to find a less precarious hold.

Carefully I levered myself onto the branch and then into a sitting position, clinging to another branch just above me for additional support. By the time Li Po clambered up to sit beside me, my heart was just beginning to settle.

"You're out of your mind. You know that, don't you?"

"You ought to know better than to issue a challenge," I reminded. However, I'd come close enough to disaster to admit, at least to myself, that Li Po was absolutely right.

Thank you, mighty dragon, I thought. Surely it had heard my prayer and helped to carry me across the stream. But I'd succeeded by no more than the reach of my fingers. Maybe I would think before I jumped next time around. There's a first time for everything, or so they say.

"Nice shot," I said, now that I had my breath back.

"Thank you," Li Po replied.

"You'll be a famous archer someday. You mark my words," I went on. "The pride of the Son of Heaven's army."

Li Po gave a snort. "Not if I can help it. Besides, you're the one who's always pining for adventure, not me. If you had your way, you'd ride off into the sunset and never look back."

I plucked a handful of leaves from a nearby branch and then released them, watching as they fluttered downward. They settled onto the surface of the water and were swiftly carried away.

"There's not much chance of that happening," I said. "I haven't got a horse of my own."

Li Po chuckled, but his eyes were not smiling. He was like this sometimes, in two places at once. It was one of the things I liked best about him. For Li Po the world was not always a simple place. It was filled with hills and valleys, with shadows and nuances.

"Where would you go?" he inquired.

"I don't know," I answered with a shrug. "I'm not even sure *where* is the point. I'd just like to be able to go. Girls don't get out much, or go very far when they do, just in case you hadn't noticed."

Li Po fell silent, gazing down into the water. "They go to their husband's homes," he said after a moment.

"Don't remind me," I said glumly. "Though I'm

never going to get married. Didn't you hear? Min Xian said your mother told her so just the other morning. According to her there's not a family in all China who'd have me, in spite of the Hua family name. I'm far too unmanageable and wild. She said that's the real reason my father hasn't come home once since the day I was born."

"The great general Hua Wei is afraid of his own daughter? That doesn't seem very likely," Li Po remarked.

"Not out of fear—out of embarrassment," I replied. I yanked the closest plum from its hold and hurled it down into the water with all my might. "Your mother told Min Xian that she prays daily to her ancestors that you won't fall in love with me."

Li Po frowned, and I knew it meant he'd heard his mother say so too. "I've heard her tell my father she wishes they could send me to Chang'an," he said. "To the home of my father's older brother."

"But I thought they *were* sending you," I said. "When you turn fifteen."

Going to the capital would help complete Li Po's education and help turn him into the scholar his family desired. If all went well, he would pass one of the grueling tests that would make him eligible for a government position. Then both he and his family would be set for life.

"That was the plan," Li Po agreed. "But now she wants to hurry things along."

"It's because of me, isn't it?" I said. Girls married at

fifteen, but most boys waited until they were older. Twenty was considered the proper age for a young man to take a wife.

"What does she think will happen? That I'll suddenly become an endless temptation? That I'll distract you from your studies?"

My chest ached with the effort I was making not to shout. The thought of me as an endless temptation, to Li Po or anyone else, was so ridiculous it should have made me laugh. So why on earth did I feel like crying?

It's because Li Po's mother is right, and you know it, Mulan, I thought. *No one is going to want you, in spite of the name of Hua. The only thing that will make it possible for you to marry is if you meet your bridegroom on your wedding day, so he doesn't have the chance to get to know you ahead of time.*

No one would want an unruly girl like me. Unlike my parents, I would not be offered the chance to marry for love.

All of a sudden I realized I was gripping the tree branch so tightly the knuckles on both hands had turned stark white.

"You can't really blame them for wanting what's best for me," Li Po said. "I'm their only son. I have to pass my examinations and marry well. It's expected, and I owe it to them, for raising me."

"In that case they're not making any sense," I snapped, completely overlooking the fact that I wasn't making much myself. "They'll have to look long and hard before they find a girl with a better family name than Hua."

"That is true," Li Po replied. "If the family name were all there was to think about. But marriage is not as simple as that, and you know it, Mulan. For example, do you really want my mother for your *popo*, your mother-in-law?"

"Of course not," I said at once. "No more than she wants me for a daughter-in-law. Or than I want you for a husband or you want me for a wife." All of a sudden a terrible doubt occurred. I twisted my head to look at Li Po more closely.

"You aren't thinking of asking me to marry you, are you?"

For the first time in our friendship I could not read Li Po's expression. Until that moment I would have said I knew any emotion he might show. Then he exhaled one long, slow breath, and I knew what his answer would be.

"Seriously?" he said. "I suppose not, no. But I'd be lying if I said I don't think about it sometimes. It would solve both our problems, Mulan. I'd have a wife who wouldn't pester me to be ambitious, to become something other than what I wanted. You'd have a husband who'd do the same for you. That wouldn't be so bad, would it?"

"No, it wouldn't," I replied.

Li Po and I had talked about many things during the course of our friendship, but we'd never really talked about the future. It had simply been there, looming in the distance, as dark and threatening as a storm cloud. Had we been hoping to make it go away by ignoring it? Or had we hoped to outrun it?

"What do you want to be?" I asked quietly, somewhat chagrined that the question had never occurred to me before now. I'd been so busy identifying the boundaries that contained me that I hadn't taken the time to see the ones that bound Li Po.

He gave a slightly self-conscious laugh. "I'm not sure I know. That's the problem. And I'm not so sure it would make any difference even if I did. Boys aren't allowed to make choices any more than girls are. I know you don't think this is so, but it's the truth, Mulan. If I go against the wishes of my family, if I bring them dishonor, everyone will suffer."

"But I thought you wanted to be a poet or a scholar," I said. "Isn't that what your family wants too?"

"It is what they want," Li Po agreed. "But how can I know if it's what I want when I've never been allowed to consider any other options? Just once I'd like to be free to listen to the voice inside my own head, to discover something all on my own.

"That's part of why I like being with you. You may be bossy . . ." He slid me a quick laughing glance to take in my reaction. "But you never boss me around. So, yes, I do wonder what it would be like to be married to you, sometimes. You'd let me be myself, and I'd do the same for you."

"And your mother?" I asked. "How would we convince her to leave us both alone?"

Li Po gave a sigh. "I don't have the faintest idea," he admitted.

"It sounds as if we should ride off into the sunset together," I said. "Very quietly, and on your horse."

"It does sound pretty silly when you put it that way, doesn't it?" Li Po said.

"Not silly," I answered. "Just impossible."

We sat quietly. The branches of the old plum tree swayed and whispered softly, almost as if they wished to console us.

"It's getting late," Li Po said finally. "I should probably be getting home. The last thing we want is for my mother to send out a search party."

"Shh!" I said suddenly, clamping a hand around his wrist to silence him. "Listen! I think someone's coming."

Above the voice of the stream, I heard a new sound—the sound of horses. Now that I'd acknowledged it was there, I realized I'd been hearing it for quite some time. But I'd been so wrapped up in my conversation with Li Po that I hadn't recognized all the other things my ears were trying to tell me.

I could identify the creak of leather, the faintest jingle of harness. And most of all, I could hear the sharp sound of horses picking their way carefully over stones.

They are coming up the streambed! I thought. *And there is more than one.* They were close. In another moment the horses would pass beneath the boughs of the plum tree that extended out over the water.

"Li Po, your legs," I whispered suddenly, for they were dangling down.

Li Po gave a frown. His head was cocked in my direction, though his eyes stayed fixed on the scene below.

"What?"

"Pull up your legs," I said, urgently now. "Whoever is coming will be able to see them. They're longer than mine."

To this day I'm not quite sure how it happened. As a general rule Li Po was no more clumsy than I. Perhaps it was the fear of being caught, the astonishment that whoever was coming had chosen to ride up the streambed rather than the road. But in his haste to get his feet up out of the way, Li Po lost his balance. He reached for a branch to steady himself. Unfortunately, he found me instead.

One moment I was sitting in the tree. The next, I was hurtling down. And that is how I came to fall from the same tree twice.

FIVE

I'd like to tell you that I fell in brave and stoic silence, but the truth is that I shrieked like an outraged cat the whole way down. I landed in the stream this time around. The impact was painful. The water wasn't deep enough to truly cushion my fall, and the streambed was full of stones.

I had no time to consider my cuts and bruises, however, because I landed squarely in the path of the lead horse. Its cry of alarm and outrage echoed my own. I scrambled to get my legs back under me, scurrying backward like a crab, kneeling on all fours. I tossed my drenched braid over my back and looked up just in time to see a pair of hooves pawing the air above me.

Every instinct screamed at me to *move*, to get out of the way. But here my mind won out. I put my arms up to shield my head and stayed right where I was. To move now would only startle the horse further. And I had no idea just where those pawing hooves might fall. If I moved, I could put myself squarely beneath them. Terrifying as it was, I had to stay still and pray that the rider would soon get the frightened animal under control.

Above the high-pitched neighing of the horse, I heard a deep voice speaking sternly yet with great calm. The voice found its way to my racing heart, steadying its beats, though they still came fast and hard.

With a final cry of outrage the horse brought his front legs down, hooves *clacking* sharply as they struck the stones of the streambed less than a hand's breadth from where I knelt. The horse snorted and danced backward a few steps before finally agreeing to stand still, the stern, soothing voice of its rider congratulating it now.

I wished the earth would open up and swallow me whole. That way I wouldn't be required to provide explanations for my behavior, nor patiently accept the punishments that would no doubt be the result. I would simply disappear, my transgressions vanishing with me as if we had never existed at all.

But since I already knew all about wishes that never came true, I did the only thing I could: I lowered my arms from shielding my face and looked up.

The horse's legs were the first thing I saw.

They were pure white, as if he'd borrowed foam from the water, and they rose up to join a glossy dark coat the color of chestnuts. He had a broad chest and bright, intelligent eyes. Though, I could see from his still-quick breathing that only the will of his rider kept him in place.

The rider, I thought.

"*Yuanliang wo*," I said, remembering my manners at long last. "Forgive me, elder."

Still kneeling in the stream, I bent over until my face was almost touching the water. I did not know who the stranger on this horse might be, but I knew enough to recognize that he had to be someone of rank—a court official, maybe even a nobleman. No ordinary man rode a horse such as this.

"I did not mean to startle your horse."

The horse blew out a great breath, as if to encourage its rider to speak. To my astonishment, it worked.

"But you did mean to fall from the tree," suggested a deep voice.

I straightened up in protest before I could help myself.

"No!" I cried. "I am a good climber. I've only fallen once before, and that was when I was much younger. This was all—"

Appalled with myself, I broke off, bowing low once more. Li Po had not fallen when I had. If I did not mention him, there was every reason to think I could keep him out of trouble.

"It's all my fault, elder," I heard Li Po say. Out of the corner of my eye I saw him march down the bank and make the proper obeisance. He'd climbed down from the tree while I was doing my best to avoid being trampled by the horse.

Oh, Li Po, you should have stayed put, I thought.

"And how is it your fault?" the stern voice asked. "I don't see you in the water."

"No, but you should," Li Po replied in a steady

voice that I greatly admired. "I was also in the tree. I was the first to lose my balance."

"What were you doing up there in the first place?" a second voice inquired. It was not as deep and powerful as the first, but it was still a voice that commanded attention.

The second rider, I thought.

"Nothing in particular," Li Po said, but his voice was less certain now.

This was not an outright lie. We hadn't been doing anything in particular. Just talking. But even this was going to be difficult to explain. Girls and boys did not usually climb trees together—especially not when they'd reached our age.

"A tree is an unusual place for doing 'nothing in particular,'" the first rider observed. His horse shifted its weight once more. "You, in the stream, stand up," he barked suddenly. "I want to get a better look at you."

This was the moment I'd been dreading. *Be brave, Mulan,* I thought. *Don't let him know that you're afraid. Remember you are a soldier's daughter.*

I stood up, trying to ignore the way water dripped from virtually every part of me. I stuck my chin out and squared my shoulders, actions I sincerely hoped would make me appear larger and braver than I actually felt. I was careful not to look into the nobleman's face. Asking to look at me was not the same as giving me permission to return the gaze. Instead I kept my eyes fixed at a spot just over the man's left shoulder.

A strange silence seemed to settle over all of us. In it I could hear the voice of the wind and the song of the stream. I could hear the nobleman's horse breathing through its great nose. I could hear my own heart pounding deep inside my chest. And I could hear my own blood rushing through my veins as if to reach some destination not even it had chosen yet. The blood that made me different, that set me apart from everyone else.

Say something! Why doesn't he say something? I thought. But it was the second rider who spoke up first.

"What is your name, child?" he inquired.

"I am called Mulan, sir," I replied.

"And your family name?" the first rider barked. His voice was strained and harsh.

"Of the family of Hua," I replied. "My father is the great general Hua Wei. He serves the emperor. And . . ." My voice trailed off, but I put my hands on my hips, planting my soaking feet more firmly in the stream. It was either this or start crying.

"You'd better watch out," I said stoutly. "If you hurt me, my father will track you down. Not that you'll be able to. I'll hurt you first, for I am not afraid of anyone!"

"Nor should you be," the second rider observed. "Not with the brave blood that flows through your veins." My ears searched for but failed to find any hint of laughter in his voice.

"Tell me something, Hua Mulan," he went on. "What does your father look like?"

"That is easy enough to answer," I replied with a snort. I was no longer cold. Instead I was warm with a false bravado that made me reckless.

"He looks just as a great general should," I went on. "He is broad-shouldered and strong, and his eyes are as keen as a hawk's. He has served the Son of Heaven well for many years. He has killed many Huns."

"Those last two are true enough, anyway," the second rider said, and as abruptly as it had swelled, my heart faltered.

He knows my father! I thought.

The second rider spurred his mount forward until the two horses stood side by side. He reached over and clapped his riding companion on the back.

"You should have come home sooner, my friend," he said. "It would seem your daughter has grown into a son."

"Huh," the first man said. It was a single syllable that could have meant anything, or nothing, but I was glad he said no more. I could hardly hear anything over the roar inside my head. "I have come home now," he said. "That must be enough."

He guided his horse forward to where I stood frozen with astonishment, and then he extended one arm. I stared at his outstretched hand as if I had never seen such an appendage.

"Get up behind me and I will take you home."

I did as he instructed. And in this way I met my father, the great general Hua Wei, for the very first time.

৴ ৴ ৴

The ride home was anything but comfortable. But if my father hoped to test my mettle, I passed with flying colors. Though I clung to his back so tightly I could feel the weave of his leather armor beneath his shirt, and though my legs gripped the great stallion's flanks so firmly and with such determination that they were sore for days afterward, I did not complain.

And I did not fall off.

My father was silent the whole way home. I imagined his disapproval of me growing stronger with every step of the horse. He had sent Li Po off with barely a word, save for extracting his name and promising to visit his family as soon as possible.

Images of the punishments Li Po might incur for trying to stand up for me tormented me until I thought my head would spin right off my shoulders. It also made me bold in a way I might not have been if I'd felt the need to defend only myself.

"You must not blame Li Po," I said as soon as we arrived at the Hua family compound. Tall as my father's horse was, I slid down from his back without assistance, firming up my knees to keep my legs steady beneath me. I could not show weakness now.

"What happened today was not his fault. It was mine."

A look that might have been surprise flickered across my father's stern features, but whether it was in reaction to my words or my actions, I could not tell.

"We will not," he said succinctly as he swung down from the horse's back himself, "have this discussion, and we will most certainly not have it here and now. I am your father. It is not your place to tell me what to do."

His right leg moved stiffly, as if it did not wish to bend.

"But I have to," I protested. "You don't know Li Po as I do. He is smart and kind. And he . . ." I felt the hitch of tears at the back of my throat. "He's my only friend. He loves me more than you do, and I won't have you hurt him."

"Mulan!" I heard Min Xian's scandalized tone. She and Old Lao had come out into the courtyard at the sound of the horses.

"You must forgive her, master," she said as she went to her knees before my father. "She doesn't know what she's saying. It's just . . . the surprise . . ."

"Of course I know what I'm saying," I snapped.

What difference did it matter what I said at this point?

The reunion I'd waited for my whole life had happened at last. I'd finally met my father, face-to-face, and he hadn't so much as batted an eye. He hadn't shown by any word or gesture that he had missed me, that he was pleased to see me, or that he wished to claim me as his own. Instead he'd made it perfectly clear that our relationship was to be one of duty and of obedience and nothing more. His coldness, his indifference, pierced me, wounding just as deeply as any sword.

"My father does not love me," I said. I went to Min Xian and knelt down beside her. "You know this, and I know it, Min Xian. In my life there have been only three people who cared for me at all. You, Old Lao, and Li Po."

I raised Min Xian to her feet, keeping an arm firmly around her waist as I lifted my eyes to my father's. To this day I cannot tell you what made me feel so strong. It was as if, having encountered my worst fears, I had nothing left to lose.

I saw the truth now. The thing I wanted most had been lost long ago, lost on the day I was born. There would be no chance to win my father's love at this late date.

"Punish me as you like," I said now. "That is your right, for I am your child. But do not punish those whose only transgression was that they did what you would not, took me into their hearts and gave me love. Surely that would be unworthy of you, General Hua Wei, for it would also be unjust."

My arm still around Min Xian, I turned to go.

"Mulan."

It was the first time I had ever heard my father speak my name. In spite of my best effort it stopped me in my tracks. Slowly I turned around.

"Yes, Father," I said. But I did not kneel down. I would meet my fate standing on my own two feet.

He will pronounce my punishment now, I thought. Perhaps I would be beaten, locked away without food, or, worst of all, forbidden to see Li Po. But it seemed the surprises of the day were not over yet.

"I will spare your friends if you answer me one question," my father said.

"What would you like to know?"

"If you could have anything you wished for, anything in all the world, what would it be?" my father asked.

If he had told me I was the loveliest girl in all of China and that he loved me, I could not have been more astonished.

Oh, Father, you are half an hour too late, I thought.

Unbeknownst to my father, he had already granted one of my wishes. He had come home. But the very arrival that had granted one wish had deprived me of another. It was clear that I could never make him proud of me. I could never earn his love. My heart had only one wish left.

"I would like to know my mother's name," I said.

Then I turned and left the courtyard.

SIX

Following the dramatic events of my father's home-coming, an uneasy peace settled over our household. Somewhat to my surprise, there was no more talk of punishment. But then there wasn't much talk of anything, in fact. For we all quickly learned that one of my father's most formidable attributes was his ability to hold his tongue.

When someone refuses to speak, those around him are left to imagine what his thoughts might be, and all too often the possibilities conjured up are not pleasant ones. It made no sense to me that my father did not back up his stern words with equally stern actions. Surely this was part of being a soldier. And so I did not trust the uneasy peace that came with this current silence.

But at least my outburst had taught me a lesson. Sometimes, no matter how much you wish to pro-claim them, it is better to keep your thoughts to yourself. Speaking out when someone else is silent puts the speaker at a disadvantage. And so I learned to hold my tongue.

It's difficult to know how things would have

resolved themselves without the help of two unexpected elements: my skill with a sewing needle and my father's traveling companion, General Yuwen Huaji.

"You must not take your father's long absence so much to heart, Mulan," he said to me one day several weeks after their arrival.

General Yuwen was my father's oldest and closest friend. They had served together for many years, commanding troops that had fought side by side as they'd battled the Huns. It was General Yuwen who had been with my father when word of my mother's death had arrived.

And my father had been in battle at General Yuwen's side not two months before we met, when his old friend had seen his only son cut down by the leader of the Huns. The fact that General Yuwen had slain the Hun leader, thereby avenging his son's death and securing a great victory for China, had not softened the blow of his loss. After a great victory celebration members of the army were given permission to go home. General Yuwen decided to accompany my father.

For some reason I could not account for, General Yuwen had taken a liking to me, which was just as well, since my father was doing his best to ignore me. The two men had just returned from spending a week touring the far corners of my father's estate, making sure everything was being run properly.

"And you must not mind that it takes him a while to grow re-accustomed to the peace and quiet of the countryside," General Yuwen continued as we walked along. "Returning here was . . . not his first choice."

I had not been permitted to see Li Po since my father's homecoming. In Li Po's absence I often took walks with General Yuwen. He quickly came to enjoy walking by the stream, and this was the route he had chosen for us this afternoon, saying he needed to stretch his legs after so many hours in the saddle. My father did not accompany us.

"Then why did he come home at all?" I asked now. "You will be returning to the emperor's service, will you not? Why should my father stay in the country?"

Surely he isn't staying because of me, I thought.

"Your father is growing older, as we all are," General Yuwen said. His words were reasonable, but I had the sense he was temporizing, working up to something else. "This is his boyhood home. He has many happy memories of this place."

"And many unhappy ones," I countered. Though perhaps they could not precisely be called memories, as my father had not physically been here on the day that I was born. "This is where my mother died."

General Yuwen was silent for several moments, reaching out to help me over a patch of uneven ground. One of my father's first edicts had been that my wardrobe had to be improved. My tunics and pants had been banished and silk dresses put in their place. They were not as fine as if I'd lived in the city, but they still took some getting used to. They were awkward and slowed me down.

"This was a lot easier when I could wear clothes like a boy's," I said.

General Yuwen smiled. "I'm sure it was, and I sympathize. Unfortunately, you are not a boy."

"I'm sure my father would agree with that sentiment," I said, the words flying from my mouth before I could stop them.

General Yuwen was quiet for several moments.

"It may not be my place to say this, Mulan," he said at last, gesturing to a fallen log. We sat down upon it, and the general stretched his long legs out in front of him. "But not all is as it seems with your father. He sustained a serious wound in our last battle with the Huns—"

"It's his right leg, isn't it?" I interrupted. General Yuwen's head turned toward me swiftly, as if in surprise, and I felt my face coloring.

"My father favors his right leg," I said. "His gait is not smooth and easy, as yours is, when he walks. Mounting and dismounting his horse seems to give him pain, and he always has more trouble walking after a ride."

"You have keen eyes," said General Yuwen. "And what's more, you use them well. Your father took a deep wound to his right thigh. The doctors stitched it up, but still it will not heal properly.

"Now that the leader of the Huns is dead and peace has been established . . ." General Yuwen paused and took a deep breath. "The emperor has given your father permission to retire to his estates."

"Retire to his estates," I echoed. "You mean the Son of Heaven sent my father home? After all those years of service, he sent him packing, just like that?"

"There is something more," General Yuwen acknowledged. "It is true that the leader of the Huns is dead. But he has a son who escaped, a son who is old enough to raise an army and return to fight us.

"The emperor believes such a possibility is unlikely. He believes the Huns have been crushed. Your father does not agree."

"Don't tell me," I said suddenly. "My father spoke his mind."

"He did." General Yuwen nodded. "The trouble is that your father gave his opinion when the emperor did not ask for it. This has made the Son of Heaven very angry, so he gave your father *permission to retire* to the country."

"I see," I said softly.

"You must not pity him," General Yuwen said quickly. "And you must be careful not to reveal what I have told you. That, I think, would make things even more tense between the two of you than they already are."

"What should I do, then?" I asked, genuinely interested.

General Yuwen clapped his palms down against his knees, a signal that we'd been sitting long enough.

"The same thing I tell him he must do for you," he said. "You must give each other time."

General Yuwen stood and reached down a hand to help me to my feet. "Now tell me about this friend of yours, Li Po."

"Why do you want to know about Li Po?" I asked, surprised.

"Answer my question first," the general said. "Then I will answer yours."

"Li Po is smart," I said. "His family wants him to be a scholar, but I told him he could be the finest archer in all of China."

"It was he who taught you to shoot?" General Yuwen inquired.

I nodded. "And to read and write, to ride, and use a sword. I offered to teach him how to embroider, but he declined."

General Yuwen smiled. "But surely you knew that for him to teach you such things, and for you to learn, was risky for you both."

"We made a pact of friendship," I said slowly. "We promised to be true to each other for the rest of our lives. Li Po wanted to share what he was being taught, and I wished to learn. I—"

I broke off, wondering how I could make him understand. "I am not like other girls, General Yuwen. I never have been, not from the day I was born. Min Xian says it's because my parents loved each other. That it's because I am a child created by true love when my parents were granted their hearts' desires. So it only makes sense that I would wish to follow my heart too."

"And what does your heart desire, Mulan?" General Yuwen asked quietly.

"To be allowed to be itself," I answered at once. "I wish to be neither more nor less than Hua Mulan. But I must be allowed to discover what that means. I think that is all Li Po wants. That's what we were talking about in the tree that day. We were trying to figure out the way to know who we are, to be true to ourselves."

"You would miss him if he went away, then?" the general asked, and I felt a band of ice close around my heart.

"I knew it. Li Po's going to be punished, isn't he?" I said. "My father is going to make sure he's sent away."

"It's not quite like that," General Yuwen said. He came to a halt again. Abruptly I realized we had walked all the way to the plum tree. We stood for a moment, gazing at its ancient boughs. The plums were long gone now. Autumn was on its way. Soon the leaves would change color and fall. The tree would change, as all living things do.

How will I change, without Li Po?

"Your father may be retired, but I am not," General Yuwen went on. "Though the country is at peace, someone must still keep a watchful eye, to safeguard China. The emperor has given me this honor."

"I congratulate you," I said.

"Thank you," General Yuwen said with a faint smile. He paused for a moment, his eyes on the plum tree. "If my son were still alive," he went on, "I would rely on him to help me. I need someone to be my aide, someone quick-witted whom I can trust, who I know is loyal.

"My son is dead," General Yuwen said softly. "But I have been thinking of your friend, Li Po."

"Li Po is all the things you describe," I said, both moved and astonished. "But you would do that? You would take Li Po into your household? Give him such an important position even though you barely know him?"

"I would," General Yuwen said. "If you thought he might wish it. The friendship of which you speak, the one the two of you share, is a very rare gift, Mulan. Someone willing to bestow such a gift should not be punished for it, nor should he be left to languish in the countryside.

"As for my trust, that is something he must earn, of course, as I must earn his devotion. But from all you have told me, I think we would both be equal to the task."

"You would never regret it," I said. "Li Po would serve you well. And I think that what you offer would make him happy."

"And what about you? Would this make you happy?"

"Yes," I answered honestly. "And no. There are times when I think I don't want anything to change. Then I remind myself they changed forever the day my father came home. But even if he had not, I am not so young and foolish that I believe Li Po and I could have gone on as we were forever. And since I am not, then I must learn to put the wishes of his heart before those of mine."

"You are most certainly not young and foolish, in that case," the general answered. "You have just given me a fine and true definition of love. I will speak to his family, then, and if all goes well, Li Po will accompany me when I depart."

"When will that be?" I inquired.

"In about a week's time. Now that your father has toured all his estate, I have helped him as he needed. It is time for me to return to the emperor's service, to the court at Chang'an."

"My father will be sorry to see you go," I said. "Though I don't think he'll say so."

"And what about you?" General Yuwen asked with a smile.

"I'll be sorry to see you go too," I said. And I meant it. "May I write to Li Po?"

"Of course you may," General Yuwen said as we turned our steps toward home. "And I'll make sure he has time to answer."

We walked in silence for several moments.

"I would like to ask you something," I said. "Though I'll understand if you don't want to tell me."

"What would you like to know?"

"Did you know my mother?" I asked in a rush. "I'm not asking you to tell me her name," I hurried on. "I'm just wondering if you knew her, if you would be willing to tell me something of what she was like."

"I did know your mother," General Yuwen said quietly. All of a sudden he stopped. I saw him look up and down the stream, as if searching for something. "Ah, there it is," he said. "Come with me, Mulan. Don't worry. I'll tell your father this was all my idea if you come home wet and muddy."

I followed General Yuwen down the bank to the stream. I thought I knew where he was going. There was a place just ahead where the stream cut into the earth to form a deep, still pool. The banks rose up steeply on either side. A narrow path led down to a shelf overhanging the pool. From it a person could kneel and look down into the water.

General Yuwen knelt and then leaned out, gesturing for me to do the same. I gazed down and saw our faces reflected below us.

"If you want to know what your mother looked like, you have only to gaze at your own face," General Yuwen told me.

Startled, I lifted a hand to my cheek, and saw my reflection do the same.

"Has no one told you?"

"No," I replied. I stared at my face. The girl in the water had high, sweeping cheekbones, a determined chin, dark and wide-spaced eyes. *It is not a beautiful face*, I thought. But it was a face that others would remember. Without vanity, I thought I could determine that much.

"Min Xian used to tell me I reminded her of my

mother," I said after a moment. "But she usually did this when I was upset about something, so I thought she was just trying to offer comfort."

"I'm sure she was," replied General Yuwen. "She was also telling you the truth. The resemblance is . . . startling."

"That explains it," I said as I sat back.

"Explains what?" asked General Yuwen.

"The day you and my father arrived," I said. "My father asked me to show my face, to look up. When I did, there was this odd silence, one I couldn't explain. But I think I understand it now. It's because you both were looking into my face and seeing my mother's."

"It was a shock, let me tell you," General Yuwen acknowledged. "Particularly since I'm pretty sure your father and I both thought you were a boy from your dress and defiance, until that moment."

General Yuwen reached out, disturbing the calm surface of the water in order to pick out a stone. He turned it over between his hands and then passed it to me. It was shaped like an egg, made smooth by the water, the perfect size to fit in the center of my palm. I closed my fingers around it, feeling its cool strength.

"Is that why my father dislikes me so much?" I asked. "Because I look just like my mother?"

"It's nothing so simple," General Yuwen said. "And I don't believe that your father dislikes you, Mulan. But looking at your face does remind him of what he has lost. I don't think that can be denied."

"But it could remind him of other things too, couldn't it?" I asked. "It could remind him of happier times."

"It could," acknowledged General Yuwen. "And I hope as he gets to know you better that that's exactly what it will do. But you must give it time, Mulan.

"I know thirteen years must seem like a very long time to grieve, but I was beside your father when word came of your mother's death. I heard his heart break in sorrow. I'm not sure there's enough time in all eternity to mend a wound like that. There is only the will and the discipline to carry on. Your father possesses those qualities in abundance.

"But holding fast to discipline makes it hard to reach for anything else, even if you wake up one day and discover you might want to."

"Why does my daughter always seem to be either in or about to fall into that stream?" I heard a deep voice inquire from behind me.

General Yuwen and I both gave a start and turned.

Hands on hips, looking as tall as a monolith, my father was standing on the bank above us.

SEVEN

"It's all my fault," General Yuwen said easily. He got to his feet and helped me to mine. "Just as it's my fault if Mulan has spoiled her fine new clothes. I wanted to show her something, and this was the best place to do it."

"Huh," my father said. This seemed to be his favorite remark. But he did not ask what General Yuwen had wanted me to see, and for this I was grateful. I hadn't yet decided how I felt about looking so much like my mother.

"You should come home to dinner," my father said now. "Min Xian wondered where you two had gone. I was afraid she would start fussing."

"By all means, let's return, then," General Yuwen said. He glanced in my direction, and I thought I saw him wink. Could my father have actually been worried about me?

"I don't know about you, Mulan, but all of a sudden I'm starving."

"Min Xian's food is always excellent," I said.

"Huh," my father said again. He turned to go. But then something unexpected happened. The bank was wet, the result of the recent rains, and as my father put his weight onto his back leg, he slipped. His leg gave way and my father fell heavily to the ground. Before either General Yuwen or I could take a step, my father was rolling down directly toward us.

General Yuwen moved swiftly, placing himself between my father and the water. There was a grunt of impact as their bodies connected, followed by a moment of silence as the two friends lay sprawled on the shelf above the water. At General Yuwen's motion I had scrambled back, out of the way. Now I moved swiftly to kneel down beside the two men. General Yuwen was the first to sit up.

"Are you all right?" I asked anxiously. My father still lay upon his back. "You're not hurt, are you?"

"Of course I'm not hurt," my father said gruffly. "It will take more than a fall to wound an old campaigner like me." He frowned suddenly, and I followed the direction of his eyes. To my shock I saw that I was holding his hand between both of my own, gripping it tightly.

My father lifted his eyes to mine.

"I thank you for your concern, Daughter," he said.

I released his hand. "You are welcome, Father."

"At least now *all* of us are muddy," General Yuwen spoke up, his voice as sunny as a spring morning.

At this my father began to roar with helpless laughter. It didn't take long before General Yuwen and I joined him. All three of us sat in the mud of the stream bank, laughing until our sides ached.

"What's the matter? Are you injured?" Over the sound of our laughter, I heard Li Po's anxious voice.

"We are not injured," my father said as he reached to wipe the tears of laughter from his eyes. Unfortunately, this only smeared more mud across his face.

"We are muddy and hungry and we are going home to eat," my father continued. "And you are coming with us. Come and help me up, Li Po."

Eyes wide in astonishment, Li Po climbed carefully down the bank. Together he and General Yuwen helped my father to his feet. But when my father went to take a step, his right leg buckled once more. Were it not for the fact that the others held his arms, he'd have collapsed to the ground.

"You *have* hurt yourself," I cried. "I'll bet the fall pulled your stitches out."

I watched my father grit his teeth against the pain. "I don't know what you're talking about."

"Oh, stop it," I said. "This is no time for heroics. You do so. Now," I went on, addressing Li Po and General Yuwen, "you help him home, being as careful of that leg as you can. I'm going on ahead to tell Min Xian to boil plenty of water. If those stitches have come out, we're going to have to sew up the wound again."

Gathering my skirts like a child playing dress-up in her mother's clothes, I sprinted up the bank and set off for home.

By the time the other three arrived, my father's

face was tight with pain and Min Xian and I had a bright fire going in the kitchen. A pot of boiling water sent up a soft cloud of steam. Li Po and General Yuwen eased my father into a chair near the fire.

"I want to see that wound," I said.

"Very well," replied my father.

A quick examination proved my worst fears. My father's fall had yanked out his stitches. "We need to clean this and then resew the wound," I said.

"I do not need to be bathed like a child," my father snapped.

I took my tongue firmly between my teeth and stepped back.

"Suit yourself," I said. "How you get that wound clean I leave to you. The new stitches you will leave to me. Min Xian's stitches would be prettier. But my eyes are stronger and my hands are steadier."

"Huh," my father said. He looked up at me for a moment, his gaze unreadable. "Huaji can clean the wound. Let's get on with it."

By the time my father's wound was clean, Min Xian and I were ready. I had passed my best sewing needle through a candle flame to sterilize it, and then I'd threaded it with a length of my strongest thread. But as I took my place at my father's side, I began to worry that my hands would shake despite all my brave words.

I stared at the gash across my father's right leg. General Yuwen had been right. The wound was not healing properly. The edges still were angry and red.

Though I knew the general had cleaned it carefully, I put a cloth into the steaming water, feeling the way its heat stung my hand. Then I pressed it to my father's wound, testing his strength and mine. The flesh of his leg quivered as if in protest to my touch, but my father never made a sound.

Just get on with it, Mulan, I thought. I set the cloth back into the dish of water and took up my needle and thread. *This is a seam, just like any other.*

Straight seams I had always been good at. Straight seams I understood. I appreciated them; they were the best way to get from here to there. It was the fancy stitches that served no purpose.

"I will hold a light for you," General Yuwen said.

"Thank you," I answered.

Li Po brought a cushion. "For your knees," he said.

I shifted back so that he could slip the cushion beneath them.

"I will begin now, if you are ready," I told my father.

"I am ready," he said.

I pulled in one deep, fortifying breath, set the needle to the edge of the wound, and began to stitch.

Afterward I was not certain how long it had taken, for time seemed first to slow and then to stop altogether. There was only the sound of my father's breathing, quick and light. General Yuwen shifted position once or twice, ever so slightly, so that my hands never worked in shadow but always in clear, bright light. And so I came to the end of the wound and knotted off the thread, snipping the extra with my embroidery scissors. I got to my feet, trying to convince myself that my knees weren't shaking.

"There. That's done," I said.

My father sat perfectly still for a moment, looking at the stitches I had made.

"It is *well* done," he said, correcting my words and praising me at the same time. Then he lifted his eyes to mine. "I thank you, my daughter."

For the first time since the day we'd met, I looked straight into my father's eyes.

"I am glad to have been of service to you," I said. "And I am happy to have pleased you, Father."

"It would please *me*," General Yuwen put in, "if you'd stay off that leg for a while. Give Mulan's fine stitches a chance to do their work."

"Why is everyone so bossy all of a sudden?" my father asked. "I'm hungry."

General Yuwen laughed, and set the lamp down. "So are we all. Let Mulan wash her hands, and then we will eat."

The four of us ate together right there in the kitchen, gathered around the fire, General Yuwen, Li Po, my father, and I. The light of the fire played over all our faces as we devoured Min Xian's good food.

It was the happiest moment of my life.

☙ ☙ ☙

General Yuwen left at the end of the week with Li Po riding beside him. Li Po promised he would write as soon as he was settled in Chang'an. I was eager to know all about the city and the duties he would perform there.

That day I awoke early, as soon as the red streaks of dawn began to mark the sky. I lit a stick of incense and said a prayer to the Hua family ancestors, asking them to watch over Li Po and General Yuwen, to keep them safe from harm. Then I put on my best dress in honor of their departure, vowing silently that I would keep it clean. I was out in the courtyard watching the sun come up when General Yuwen found me.

"Good day to you, Hua Mulan," he said. "Are you making the sun rise?"

"You are the one doing that, I think," I answered with a smile. "For she wants to keep an eye on you, to see you safely back to Chang'an."

"Thank you for your kind words," the general said. "Will you walk with me to the stables, Mulan? There is a gift I would like to give you, if you will accept it."

"With pleasure," I said.

We walked to the stables in companionable silence.

General Yuwen's horse gave a whicker of greeting at the sight of us. The general produced a slice of apple from a hidden fold in his garments, offering it on a flat palm. Then he went to where his saddlebags lay ready to be strapped to the horse's sides. General Yuwen took something from among them and then turned back to me. I caught my breath.

It was a bow. The finest I had ever seen, the wood so smooth it seemed to glow. He held it out.

"Let me see you try it," the general said.

I took it from him, feeling the weight of it in my hands. *He did not have this made for me,* I thought. I could tell that this bow had been designed for someone taller and stronger than I was. But I had no doubt I would be able to make it shoot true, if I practiced enough. Li Po had taught me to shoot using his own bow.

I set my feet, as Li Po had taught me, lifted the bow, and pulled the string back, taut. I held it there until my shoulders sang with the effort it took to hold the string straight and still. Then I eased it forward again, lowering the bow.

"That was well done," General Yuwen said. "I knew I had made a good choice." He turned back to the saddlebags and produced a quiver of fine-tooled leather filled with arrows. "These belonged to my son."

My mouth dropped open before I could stop it. "Oh, but," I stammered. "Surely Li Po . . ."

"Li Po is as fine an archer as I have seen," the general agreed. "You were absolutely right on that point. Nevertheless, I am giving this to you, Mulan. I would like you to have something to remember me by. But more than that . . ."

He paused, and took a breath. "I would like to give you something to help you to remember yourself. To remember the dreams that you hold in your heart. I will be taking Li Po far away from here, and as a result you will be lonely. Perhaps this will help."

"It is a wonderful gift," I said. "I will take good care of it, I promise. But I don't have anything to give you in return."

"You are giving me your best friend," the general said. "I think that's more than gift enough. Now let's go inside for breakfast before your father begins to fear that I intend to take you with me as well."

And so on a fine autumn morning I watched my oldest friend and my newest friend ride away together. And I wondered what would happen to those of us who stayed behind.

EIGHT

My days with my father soon fell into a rhythm. While he spoke no more than he had before, his silence no longer stung me with imagined comparisons between the daughter he had envisioned and the daughter he had actually found. This new silence felt gentler, more companionable somehow. As if my ability and determination to restitch his wound had enabled more than just the healing of his leg. It had created the possibility for us to heal as well.

I caught my father watching me from time to time when he thought I wouldn't notice. He did this mostly in the mornings while I worked dutifully at my sewing. Sometimes I wondered if it was because I looked like my mother once had, hard at work with her own needle and thread. But although my father and I were slowly drawing closer, we both avoided the subject of my mother.

My days were not all given over to traditional tasks, as I had once feared they might be. My father suggested I continue with my reading and writing. He set me a series of tests during our first days together, as if to judge my progress.

"Your friend Li Po taught you well," he commented after reviewing my work. "You have a fine and steady hand with a calligraphy brush."

"Thank you, Father," I answered, both astonished and pleased by the compliment.

My father gazed at the characters I had made, as if reading something there I had not written that only he could decipher.

"You must miss him very much," he finally said.

"Yes, I do," I said. "But I . . ." I broke off, hesitating.

My father looked up from his study of my work. "But what, Mulan?"

"I am glad that General Yuwen wanted to make Li Po his aide," I said. "It is a wonderful opportunity. It is perfect for him. I would not have you think—I wouldn't wish Li Po back just because I miss him. I am not jealous of his good fortune or his happiness."

My father regarded me steadily for several moments. It was long enough for me to curl my toes inside my shoes, the closest I could come to squirming without giving myself away.

"Your feelings do you credit, Mulan," my father said at last. "I think . . ." Now he was the one to pause, as if he wished to use the perfect words or none at all.

"I think that you would be a good friend to have."

Before I could think of an answer, my father tapped the sheet of paper in front of me with the end of his brush.

"Now," he said, "let us see if we can pick up where you and Li Po left off."

And so my father became my new teacher, teaching me even more characters than Li Po had. Surely there was not a girl in all of China with my skills, and not simply because I could read and write.

It took some time for me to decide what to do about General Yuwen's gift of his son's bow, quiver, and arrows. But I finally came to the conclusion that he had not bestowed such a gift only to have it collect dust. And so late one afternoon, as my father was following his usual custom of quiet contemplation out in the sunlight, I took General Yuwen's gift from its hiding place and changed from one of my new dresses back into my tunic and pants. Then I headed to the old plum tree.

There were no plums at this time of year, but there were still plenty of leaves to use for targets. The fact that I had learned to shoot on one of Li Po's bows now came in handy, as it meant I was accustomed to handling a bow made for someone larger than I am. I made myself string and unstring the bow half a dozen times, testing my strength against its weight before I so much as looked at an arrow. And even then I tested the tension of the string first, pulling it back, holding it steady, easing it forward another half a dozen times. Only when I felt certain that the bow and I understood each other did I select an arrow and put it to the string.

I set my feet the way Li Po had always shown me,

feeling the power of the ground beneath my feet. I pulled back the string, sighted, and then let the arrow fly. By a hand's breadth it missed my intended target, a fat cluster of autumn-colored leaves at the end of one of the plum tree's branches. Annoyed with myself, I made a rude sound. I took a second arrow and tried again. This one just tickled the leaves as it whisked by. My third arrow passed straight through the target, scattering greenery as it went. I lowered the bow and rolled my aching shoulders.

"That is fine shooting," I heard my father say. Startled, I spun around. I had been so engrossed in mastering my new bow that I hadn't heard my father approach. We stood for a moment, gazing at each other. I was just opening my mouth to apologize for both acting and looking so unladylike, when my father spoke first.

"May I see the bow?" he inquired.

Wordlessly I brought it to him. He took it in both hands and examined it closely. "I know this bow," he said at last. "It belonged to Yuwen Zhu, General Yuwen's son."

"General Yuwen gave it to me as a parting gift," I said.

"Huh," my father said, and I felt my heart plummet. In my experience this was the reply he gave when he wished to keep his feelings a secret.

"Today is the first day you have used this?" my father asked.

I nodded. "Yes, *Baba*."

Without warning my father lifted the bow as if to shoot it himself, pulling back the string.

"Huh," he said once more. He lowered the bow and turned to look at me. "And you shot only twice before you found your mark?"

"I shot three times," I said, "and found my mark on the third try. The bow and I are still becoming acquainted."

"Hmm," my father said. I wasn't quite sure what to make of this new comment.

"I suppose it was your friend Li Po who taught you to shoot as well."

"Yes, Father," I said again, and then I decided it might be better to get it all over with at once. "And to ride a horse, and to use a sword, though I'm better at riding and archery than at swordsmanship."

"Is that so?" said my father.

"I'm sorry to have deceived you," I began, "but I—"

My father held up a hand, and I fell silent. "I don't think 'deception' is quite the right word," he said quietly. "I never asked if you could do such things, for it never occurred to me that you might be able to. When I was away, I didn't think much at all about what you might or might not do, to tell you the truth."

An expression I had never seen before came and went in his eyes, too quickly for me to be able to identify it.

"Is there anything else that I should know about?"

"No," I answered as steadily as I could. "At least, I don't think so."

"So let me see if I have this right," my father went on. "I have a daughter who can read, write, ride a horse, wield a sword, and accurately shoot an arrow with a bow that would make a strong young man work hard. She can also weave, sew as fine a seam as I have ever seen, and embroider."

"Yes," I said, "but I hate the embroidery."

"I am glad to hear it," my father answered without missing a beat. "In my experience those who are good at everything usually are also good at being insufferable."

I opened my mouth, and then closed it without making a sound. "I don't know what to say," I confessed.

At this my father laughed aloud. And suddenly the expression on his face that I had been unable to read before made perfect sense. It was amusement.

He handed me back my bow. "That makes two of us, Mulan. I don't know what to say to you most of the time. That's the plain truth." He made a gesture. "Come, let's walk and retrieve your arrows."

"What about the bank?" I asked. It had been a tumble down the stream bank that had reopened his wound.

"I believe I have mended well enough to risk the stream bank," my father answered, with just the glimmer of a smile. "Mending me is something else you did well, my daughter."

We crossed the stream and retrieved my arrows in silence. My father turned and looked up into the branches of the plum tree.

"You like this place, don't you?" he asked. "You come here often."

"It's my favorite place," I answered. "It has been ever since I was a child. I don't know quite why."

My father was silent, his eyes on the tree. The leaves were turning color. Soon they would begin to fall. In less than a month I would turn fourteen. Within the following year I would be considered a young woman, old enough to marry, no longer a child.

"Your mother loved this place." My father finally spoke, his tone quiet. The gentlest breath of wind could have knocked me over in surprise.

"When your mother and I were first married, it was early spring and there was still snow on the ground. But when it melted and the plum trees began to bloom, your mother went out every day to cut branches and bring the blossoms indoors. If ever there was a moment when I could not find her, I knew right where to look. This tree was the one she loved best of all."

"It's always the first to bloom," I heard my own voice say. "Every year. I know because I watch for it." I went on, before I lost my nerve, "I'm sorry for what I said before. When you asked me what my wish might be. I was angry."

"Perhaps you had a right to be," said my father.

"That doesn't make any difference," I replied. "In my anger I spoke with disrespect. It was wrong, and I apologize."

My father pulled in a very deep breath, and expended it in a long sigh. Then, at last, he took his eyes from the tree and looked at me.

"Thank you, Mulan. You have spoken the truth to me, even though you were afraid to, I think. In return I would like to tell you a truth of my own. It is a truth that may not be easy for you to hear."

"I will listen to your words with patience, Father," I said.

My father's gaze returned to the plum tree.

"I thought that I would never return to this place," he said quietly. "I did not wish to, after your mother died. I have been a soldier almost all of my life. I have seen death. I have taken away life. Death on the battlefield is something I understand. It may not be easy, but if one dies performing his duty, a soldier dies an honorable death."

He paused, falling silent for so long I thought perhaps he did not mean to continue.

"But your mother's death, the fact that she should lose her life bringing a new one into the world . . . *That* I could not find a way to reconcile," my father went on. "I could not even find a way to honor your mother in my memory. Every thought of what we had once shared and what I had lost was like a knife twisting in my heart. I even . . ."

His voice sank so low that I had to strain to hear it. "I even wondered whether or not I might have been to blame."

"But how can that be?" I protested at once. "You

never meant her harm. You loved each other."

"But that's just it," my father said, his voice anguished now, an anguish that came from deep within him. It seemed to cause him physical pain to bring it forth. His voice sounded as if it was being wrenched from his body against his will.

"Perhaps there is a reason our people marry first and hope love will come later, rejoicing if it comes at all. Perhaps to love as strongly as your mother and I did was unnatural. Her untimely death has always seemed so."

"No," I objected. "I don't think that can be right, *Baba*. As long as you act with honor in her memory, isn't love honored also?"

"But what if I did not act with honor?" asked my father. "I locked away my feelings for your mother. I deliberately put from my mind all thoughts of this place, our lives together, and the child we had created. I told myself that I was doing what a soldier should, that I was being strong.

"But the truth is, I was doing just the opposite. I took the coward's way out, because to deny my past with your mother meant that I denied you as well. It was many years before I saw the truth of this, and by the time I did . . ."

My father broke off, shaking his head. "By the time I did, it seemed it had to be too late, as you were nearly grown."

"And then you were wounded, and you had to return here," I said, filling in the rest of the story. "And the daughter you weren't so sure you wanted fell out of a tree at your feet."

"Yes, but not just any tree," my father said, bringing us full circle. "This one. The tree your mother loved so much. That is the reason Huaji and I rode along the streambed. I wanted to see this plum tree before anything else, and you cannot see it from the road.

"And it isn't true that I did not want you, Mulan. I just didn't understand how much I did until I came home."

"Then you aren't disappointed in me?" I asked, trying to ignore the sudden quaver in my voice. "You don't . . ." I paused and took a moment to steady myself. If my father could speak of things that pained him, then so could I.

"You don't mind that I'm not like other girls too much? You don't think I will bring the family dishonor?"

"Of course not," said my father at once, and so swiftly that I knew he spoke from his heart. "I will admit you surprised me, at first."

He smiled again, ruefully this time, so I knew he was smiling at himself.

"Actually, you surprise me all the time. But being different is not necessarily a bad thing, though it can be . . . uncomfortable. When you are different, you carry a burden others may not. All of us carry the burden of our actions, since that is how we ensure that we act with honor. But when you are different, you also carry the burden of others' judgments. And many are quick to judge, and judge harshly, Mulan. You would do well to remember that."

"I will do my best, *Baba*," I promised.

"Well, then," my father said, "that is all that I can ask." He handed me back the arrows he had retrieved. "It's getting late. Let's go back to the house."

In that moment the question of my mother's name quivered on the tip of my tongue. I took my tongue firmly between my teeth and bit down. My father had shared things today I had never imagined he would. It had not been easy for him. If my father could do something difficult, then so could I. And so I did not ask the question that still burned in my heart. Instead I matched my footsteps to my father's.

We were about halfway home when we saw a figure running toward us.

"What on earth?" my father exclaimed.

"That is Old Lao," I said, beginning to feel alarmed. Never, in all the years that I had known him, had I seen Old Lao move so quickly. "Something must be wrong."

We quickened our pace, as much as my father's stiff leg would allow. When he saw us hurrying toward him, Old Lao paused. He bent over, hands on his knees, in an effort to catch his breath.

"Master and young mistress, come quickly," he gasped out as we approached. "There has been an accident. You are needed at the house."

"Run ahead and find out what it is, Mulan," my father instructed, laying a reassuring hand on my shoulder. "Old Lao and I will follow together. We will come as quickly as our legs allow."

I handed my father the bow and then took off at a dead run. And suddenly, even in the midst of my concern, I was glad to be just as I was. Glad to be different from other girls. For my father had sent me on ahead. He had given me his trust.

NINE

When I got to the house, Min Xian was fussing like a mother hen. A young noblewoman's transport had overturned in the road. One of her bearers had a broken arm. And though the lady herself was not injured, she was distressed and shaken. Min Xian sent me to comfort the young woman while Mix Xian herself prepared to set the servant's broken arm.

"You be nice now," Min Xian instructed. "No frightening her with your sudden ways. She's a real lady, and she's had a tough time."

"Of course I'll be nice," I answered, stung. "You don't need to remind me about the courtesy due a guest."

Annoyed, I stomped off. Outside the door to the great room, the one where my father and I did our lessons, I took a moment to compose myself. Coming into the room with a scowl on my face would hardly be the way to comfort a guest in distress.

"Good evening to you, mistress," I said as I entered.

The young woman was sitting at the window, but her eyes were focused downward, at the hands clasped tightly in her lap. She lifted her head at the sound of my voice, and I caught my breath.

She was the loveliest woman I had ever seen, no more than a few years older than I was. I had a swift impression of delicate features, gorgeous and elaborate clothes. I bowed low in welcome, and it was only as I did this that I realized I was wearing my old tunic and pants.

No wonder Min Xian had warned me not to frighten her, I thought. Our guest would probably think I was a boy.

"I am sorry for your troubles," I said in what I hoped was a quiet and soothing voice, resisting the impulse to smooth out my well-worn garments. "I hope you will find peace in our home. My father will be here in a moment. In the meantime, how may I see to your comfort?"

The young woman cleared her throat. "My servant," she said in a light, musical voice.

"He is being attended to as we speak," I replied. I gave her what I hoped was a reassuring smile. "You must not worry. Nobody sets bones better than Min Xian. She's getting on in years—she'd admit to this herself—but she's still strong. She'll have your servant's arm set right and bandaged in no time, just you wait and see."

The young woman's face became pale, as if just the thought of what it might take to set an arm was more than she could bear to contemplate. She had the finest skin that I had ever seen. In her bright silks she reminded me of some exotic bird that would be painted on a piece of porcelain.

"May I bring you some tea?" I asked. "Or something else that you might like? My name is Hua Mulan, by the way," I added.

"Hua Mulan?" she echoed, a faint frown appearing between her brows. "Oh, but I thought . . ." She broke off, a blush spreading across her cheeks so that now she looked like a rosebud that was just about to open. I felt a corresponding heat in my cheeks, but doubted I resembled a flower in any way.

"I'm sorry my clothes are so deceiving," I said, deciding an explanation might help. "I've been practicing my archery, and I can't wear a dress, you know, because of the sleeves . . ."

My voice trailed off as I watched our guest's eyes widen. It could have been in surprise, but it looked an awful lot like alarm.

Shut up, Mulan, I told myself. I felt like a clumsy oaf before this elegant stranger. *You're not helping things at all. When will you learn that when in doubt, it's better to hold your tongue?*

Fortunately for all concerned I was saved by the sound of approaching voices and footsteps.

"That will be my father," I said quickly. "Hua Wei. I'm sure he'll want to make sure you have everything you need."

The young woman rose gracefully to her feet just as my father came into the room.

"I am sorry for your misfortune," my father said as

he bowed in greeting. "Please make use of our humble home."

"Thank you for your kindness," the young woman answered, executing a bow of her own.

How graceful she is, I thought. *Like a willow bending in the breeze.*

"Your servant is resting," my father continued as he gestured for the young woman to resume her seat. "He will be sore for many days, but he will mend well. No one sets bones better than Min Xian."

"So your . . . daughter has told me," she replied. I felt my cheeks flush once more at the slight hesitation before the word "daughter."

"I will go and change, Father, if I may," I said.

"Of course, Mulan," my father answered without turning his head. All his attention was for the young noblewoman.

"If you will excuse me, mistress," I went on.

She did not speak, but inclined her head.

"My distress has made me forget my manners," I heard her tell my father as I made my way across the room. "I apologize. I have not introduced myself. I am Chun Zao Xing."

I tripped over the threshold and turned to stare.

"Mulan," my father said, "are you all right? Is something wrong?"

"Nothing but my own clumsiness," I answered. "Please forgive me." Then I turned and fled.

Our visitor had the same name I had given to my mother so long ago: Morning Star.

TEN

As quickly as it had arrived, the newfound close-
ness between my father and me departed—for
Zao Xing's presence changed everything in our
house. My father and I no longer had our calligraphy lessons together. He paid me no additional
visits while I practiced target shooting. Instead his
time was given over to caring for Zao Xing's comfort. Even Min Xian seemed to think this was the
proper thing to do.

"Poor thing," she remarked one morning about a
week after Zao Xing's arrival.

Her servant was healing just as he should, but
mending a broken arm takes time. My father had sent
a message to Zao Xing's family, explaining what had
transpired. In it he'd told them that their daughter
would be well cared for in our home for as long as she
and her family wished her to stay.

"I doubt they'll be in any hurry to have her back,"
Min Xian went on with a click of her tongue.

We were sitting in the kitchen working on a pile
of mending. I was happy to have something to keep
my hands busy, even if the task did keep me indoors.

"Why do you say that?" I asked, curious in spite of myself.

I could not decide how I felt about Zao Xing. It wasn't quite accurate to say that I disliked her. But I did feel very keenly when I was in her company all the ways that we were different, and the contrast made me uncomfortable.

Zao Xing had the finest dresses I had ever seen. Her hair was always elaborately styled. Her slippers were covered with embroidery stitches so tiny that just looking at them made my fingers ache. Beside her I felt like a simple country girl. Which, I suppose, is precisely what I was.

"Has your father not told you?" asked Min Xian. She went on before I could tell her what we both already knew she knew: My father had told me nothing. "Zao Xing is a young widow."

Min Xian made a sympathetic sound. "Just barely married, poor thing, when her husband's horse threw him and he broke his neck before she could conceive a child. Zao Xing's *popo*, her mother-in-law, does not love her, and a daughter-in-law who can produce no son is no use to anyone. So her husband's family was sending her back to her parents when the accident happened, right outside our door."

"That is terrible," I agreed.

To be passed around like a piece of fruit on a plate—one last, spoiled piece that nobody wanted. No wonder Zao Xing always seemed so sad, in spite of her luxurious clothes. No wonder she seemed to start at even the slightest sound, something I had found both perplexing and irritating about her. No doubt Zao Xing feared any new noise was a fresh disaster headed her way.

"Your father has his eye on her. You mark my words," Min Xian said.

"What?" I asked, my attention snapping back to Min Xian. "What did you just say?"

"I'm saying you should keep your own eyes open, that's all," said Min Xian. "Your father has been alone a long time, and a lovely young woman like that . . . You can tell he feels for her. You can see it in his face."

"I don't want to talk about this," I said.

Min Xian put down the shirt she'd been mending and regarded me steadily for several moments. She extended her hands. I placed mine into them, and she gripped me tightly.

"I know you don't, my little one. But you'll thank me for these words later. This much I have learned, in my long life. It's better to be prepared."

Then she let me go and made her favorite shooing motion. "Now go on outdoors before the sun goes down. Being in the fresh air will do you good. Don't stay out too long, though. It's turning cold."

For once I went somewhere other than the plum tree, choosing instead to walk through one of the great stands of bamboo that grew near our home. A bamboo grove is an eerie place because it always seems that the long and supple stalks speak to one another. Even when I can barely feel the breeze upon my face, the bamboo quivers. Its papery leaves hiss and rustle. Usually, I find this lack of peace unsettling. That night it was precisely what I wanted.

Could Min Xian be right? I wondered. *Does my father, who so mourned my mother that he forbade anyone to speak her name aloud, now intend to replace her with a new wife, with Zao Xing? Am I, who have been motherless all my life, about to acquire a stepmother?*

I paused before a thick stalk of bamboo and placed my hand upon it. It was smooth and cool to the touch. And suddenly, almost before my mind knew what my body intended, I leapt upward, wrapping both hands around the stalk. My weight carried us back down to earth. The leaves hissed as if in protest, the stalk strained against my hands, longing to spring free, to be upright once more. I set my feet and held on tight.

I must learn to be like this bamboo, I thought. I must learn to be stronger than I looked, so strong that I could bear a weight greater than any I had previously imagined upon my back, upon my shoulders, and in my heart. *I must learn to bend beneath my burden like the bamboo does.*

Unlike the brittle branches of a plum tree, a stalk of bamboo will not snap. The only way to break it is with the blade of a knife. That's how strong, how flexible, it is. *And I must learn to be just like it,* I thought once more. *I must learn to bend, not break.*

I let go of my hold, stepping back quickly as the

stalk of bamboo whipped upright and then seesawed from side to side before settling into its own rhythm once more.

I do not want my father to marry Zao Xing, I thought.

If he did, surely any chance he and I might have to truly come to know and understand each other would be lost. My father would have a new life, begin a new family, and it seemed all too likely there would be little room in it for me.

"There you are, Mulan," came my father's voice.

I took a moment to compose myself before turning to face him, for I did not want my father to read the conflict in my face, the worry and unhappiness in my eyes.

"I went to the plum tree," my father continued when I did not reply. An awkward silence fell. *It must be settled between them, then,* I thought. I had come to know my father's silences well.

There was the silence that spoke of his displeasure, the absentminded silence, the silence that told me he was so deep in thought that he hadn't even noticed me at all. But never before had any of my father's silences told me he was uncertain, unsure of what to do next. I listened to the great dry whisper as the wind moved through the leaves of the bamboo.

"What is it, *Baba?*" I asked quietly.

My father sighed, adding his breath to the air that stirred the great green stalks around us.

"You are absolutely right, Mulan. I did come to

tell you something, and now that I'm here, I don't know how to do it."

"Then let me guess," I said, never feeling more grateful to Min Xian than I did at that moment. Thanks to her, I would not be taken by surprise. "You are going to marry Zao Xing."

"That's right," my father said, surprise and relief both plain in his face. "How did you know?"

"I didn't," I confessed. "It was Min Xian. She was the one who said she could see how things would go."

"But you can see it does make sense," my father said, as if trying to convince us both. "To be sent back to her family like that . . ."

"I can see why any man would wish to marry Zao Xing," I answered honestly. "Just as I can see why she would wish to be your wife. It will be a fine thing for her, to become a member of the Hua family."

The only thing I could not see was where I would fit in, but this information I kept to myself.

"You will not mind too much, then?" my father asked, and here, at last, he did take me by surprise.

He is trying to break this news as gently as he can, I thought. It was a far cry from our first meeting.

"No, Father," I said. "I will not mind too much."

"Then you have made my happiness complete, Mulan." My father gave me a great surprise then, moving toward me to lay a hand upon my shoulder. It was the closest we had ever come to an embrace.

"Come," he said. "Let us return. I know Zao Xing is waiting anxiously."

My father dropped his arm but stayed beside me all the way back to the house. And so before the month was out, my life changed yet again. I turned fourteen, one year shy of being an adult myself, and Zao Xing became my stepmother.

We tried to get along, the two of us. Honestly we did. I often thought things might have been easier if we hadn't been trying quite so hard to like each other. But nothing Zao Xing and I did quite closed the gap between us. Nothing could erase how very different we were. It was as if we were speaking the same language but the words meant something different in her mouth than they did in mine. Try as we both might, we simply could not understand each other.

"We've got to do something about your clothes, Mulan," Zao Xing said after she and my father had been married for several months. "And it's high time you began to wear your hair up. You'll be married yourself in just another year."

"I sincerely hope not," I said before I could help myself.

Zao Xing turned from where she had been fussing with the contents of my wardrobe, surprise clear on her face.

"Oh, but I thought . . . your friend, the one to whom you write . . . the one General Yuwen took into his household."

"You mean Li Po?" I inquired. I had had several letters from my friend by now. Life in Chang'an was so full that Li Po claimed he worked from morning till night, but I could tell that he was enjoying himself. Serving General Yuwen was a great honor.

Lately, though, Li Po had written that there were disturbing rumors of a new threat from the Huns. It seemed that my father had been right after all. The son of the previous leader was rousing his people, claiming he had had a vision that his destiny was to avenge his father's death by leading an army to destroy China. It was said he meant to attack soon, despite the fact that winter was fast approaching.

The Emperor has called his advisers together, Li Po had written, *"trying to decide on a course of action, to determine which of the whispers racing through the city are true and which are false.*

Not even the Huns had yet tried to attack when the winter snows were this close, but it was said that the Hun leader's vision had portrayed him and his warriors lifting their swords in victory over a field of snow stained red with Chinese blood.

The peace my father and General Yuwen had spent so many years trying to achieve could end at any time.

"Li Po's mother hates me," I said simply, pulling my attention back to the conversation with my stepmother. "I think I would rather die an old maid than have her for a mother-in-law."

I watched as Zao Xing digested this information. "Oh," she said after a moment. "That is very unfortunate."

"Oh, I don't know," I answered with a sigh. "I don't particularly want to get married, to tell you the truth. I'd rather stay at home."

"Do you really mean that?" Zao Xing asked, a tone in her voice I couldn't quite read. "You would rather stay here than have a household of your own to run someday?"

"I think I do mean it," I answered slowly. "I think I would rather stay in my father's house, if I cannot do what my parents did and marry for love."

I had not intended to speak of this, for such thoughts had only begun to take shape in my mind. But now that I had said the words, I recognized them for the truth. I would rather stay alone than marry as Zao Xing once had.

"But of course I will do as my father wishes," I said. The decision of my marriage would be his, not mine.

"But if we could convince him," Zao Xing said, abandoning my clothing to move to my side. "Together, you and I. If you stayed . . . If you and I could learn to be friends. I would so like to have a true friend, Mulan. Someone who could be with me when . . ."

She blushed and broke off.

"You're going to have a baby, aren't you?" I said.

Zao Xing nodded. "I only became certain a few days ago. I haven't even told your father yet. It's my plan to do so after dinner, tonight."

She reached out and took my hands. The color in her face was bright, and her dark eyes were shining. *She is truly happy*, I thought.

"You love him, don't you?" I asked suddenly. "That's the real reason you married him."

"Of course I wanted to marry your father," Zao Xing said. "Any woman would be honored to become a member of the family of Hua."

"That's not what I mean," I said. "You *love* my father, Zao Xing. Don't deny it."

To my astonishment tears filled my stepmother's eyes. "I suppose you think that's ridiculous, don't you?" she said. "That I'm not worthy, not after the way he felt about your mother."

"Of course I don't think that," I said at once, and watched her tears spill down her cheeks. "And I know less about my mother than I do about you. I've never even heard her name."

Zao Xing let go of my hands to wipe her cheeks with an embroidered handkerchief. "So it's true. Your father forbade anyone from speaking your mother's name aloud."

"Yes, it's true," I answered quietly. "From the day of her death to this one, no one has spoken my mother's name, not even Min Xian, who nursed her when she was a child."

"Your father must have loved her very much," Zao Xing said.

"I believe he did," I answered honestly. "But I also think . . ." I paused and took a breath. "I think that he loves *you* now."

"Do you really think so?" Zao Xing asked, and I heard the yearning in her voice, the hope. "Why? I tell myself he does one minute, and then I tell myself I'm being foolish the next. Your father and I have been married only a few months. We barely know each other."

"But that's the way love is supposed to happen, isn't it?" I asked. "Out of nothing, growing over time."

I took a moment to consider why I thought my assessment of my father's feelings was correct.

"My father's face grows peaceful when he looks at you," I finally continued. "When he speaks, his voice sounds more gentle than it did before. I've never had anyone love me, not in the way we're talking about, but if someone were to offer me these gifts, I would think they were given out of love."

Zao Xing was silent for many moments, gazing at me with dark and thoughtful eyes.

"I wasn't sure that I would like you at first," she confided. "You seemed so different, so strong. I thought you would despise me for not being more like you."

"No," I said. "That's not the way things are at all. In fact, you've got it turned around. I thought you'd dislike me because we seem so unalike. I'm not pretty, and I don't know the first thing about dressing well."

"Outside things are easy to learn," my stepmother said at once. "And as for not being pretty . . ." She cocked her head to one side. Then, to my surprise, she reached out to lay a gentle palm against my cheek. "I think you have more beauty than you know. The right eyes will see your strength for the beauty that it is."

I lifted one of my hands to cover hers. "Stop it," I said. "Or you'll make me cry."

"So we're agreed, then?" Zao Xing asked. She gave my cheek a pinch that made us both smile.

"I'll tell your father about the baby tonight. And I'll say that you confided in me, that you asked me to tell your father you have no wish to be married, to leave home. Instead you'd rather remain here with us."

I nodded, to show that I agreed with this plan.

"You can help with the children, ride and shoot that enormous bow as often as you want," my stepmother went on, describing my future life. "You can give the children lessons, even the girls, when the time comes. It won't be quite like having a household of your own, Mulan, but it would not be a bad life."

"No," I answered. "Not a bad life."

I wouldn't have the respect a well-married woman would enjoy. And the children I would watch grow up would not be my own. But I would be free to be myself, loved for who I was. Wasn't that what both Li Po and I had wanted, right before I fell out of the plum tree at my father's feet? Right before my father's sudden appearance had changed all our lives?

"I gave my mother a name once," I said. "Right after my seventh birthday, when Li Po first offered to teach me to read and write. Li Po said I should give her a name I chose myself, since no one could tell me what her true one was.

"So I chose the most beautiful name I could imagine. A name that I could whisper before I fell asleep at night and when I woke up first thing in the morning. A name that could belong to any hour of the day or night, that would always bring me joy and comfort."

"What name did you choose?" my stepmother asked.

"Your name, Zao Xing," I answered softly. "I will be content to stay here if you will be content to have me."

"With all my heart," Zao Xing replied. "I will learn to be both mother and friend if you will let me. Someday I hope we may both speak the name of the woman who gave birth to you."

"I hope so too," I said.

And for the first time since I had heard the sound of horses beneath the plum tree, I felt like I was home.

ELEVEN

Less than a week later messengers sent by the emperor rode though the countryside. The rumors of a Hun attack were true. Our ancient enemy was massing in great number. In response the Son of Heaven was assembling a force to resolve the matter once and for all. A force so strong no invading army would be able to stand against it. A force that would free China from the threat of the Huns for all time.

To achieve this the emperor had commanded that every household in China send a man to fight. Recruits would meet in a great valley near the mountain pass through which it was believed the Huns would attack.

The muster would occur in one week's time.

I do not think I will ever forget the look on Zao Xing's face when the messenger arrived at our door. Never did I respect or love her more. I could see Zao Xing's body quiver with the effort it took to not cling to my father, to keep her fear and despair to herself. Not once did she beg my father to stay with her and the unborn child she carried. Not once did she plead with him to not allow history to repeat itself.

Instead she, Min Xian, and I worked together to make sure my father would have everything he needed when he rode away to war. We sewed a fur lining inside his cloak, for he was heading north and the weather would be cold.

We made sure the leather of his armor was waterproof and supple. My father cared for his weapons and his horse himself. And all of us waited for special word from the emperor calling my father to return to his duties as a general. Surely, after all Hua Wei had done to defend China, the Son of Heaven would request my father's experience once more.

But the days came and went, and no message from the emperor arrived. And though he tried to hide his pain at this, it seemed to me that with every day that passed my father grew older before my eyes. Until finally the night before he had to depart arrived. By then we all knew the truth: There would be no special summons. When my father went to fight, it would be as a common soldier. This increased the chance that he would not come back alive.

We ate a quiet dinner the night before my father's departure. Zao Xing's eyes were red, signaling she had been crying in private. But she sat at my father's side and served him his dinner with her customary grace.

From across the table I watched the two of them together. I saw the way my father angled his body toward her as he sat, a gesture I think he made without knowing it. I saw the way their fingers met as she passed him dishes, lingered for a few moments before moving on to their next task.

They are showing their love for each other without words, I realized suddenly. And though I was sure they would do so later in the privacy of their own apartments, it seemed they were also saying good-bye. As I watched them demonstrate their love, I felt a resolution harden in my heart. It was one that had been taking shape there for many days, ever since word of the muster had come, but that I had allowed myself to clearly acknowledge only that night.

I cannot let him go, I thought.

My father had as quick and agile a mind as ever, a mind that could have been used against the Huns. But his body was growing old. The wound that had sent him home in the first place had been slow to heal. There was every reason to suppose my father would not survive another injury. Against all odds he had found happiness. My father had a new, young wife who would give him a child, perhaps even a son.

If I had been a son, I could have gone to fight in my father's place. My father could have remained home and our family could still have kept its honor. But I was not a boy; I was a girl. A girl who could ride a horse, with or without a saddle. A girl who could shoot an arrow from a bow made for a tall, strong man and still hit her target. A girl who had never wanted what other girls want. A girl unlike any other girl in China.

I must not let my father go to fight, I thought. *I will not.*

I would not watch my father ride away, and then stay behind to comfort my stepmother as she cried herself to sleep at night. I loved them both too much. And I had waited too long for my father to come home in the first place to stand in the door of our home now and watch him ride away to die.

And so I would do the only thing I could to protect both my father's life and our family's honor: I would go to fight in his place. I would prove myself to be my father's child, even if I was a daughter.

I waited until the house was quiet and then waited a little longer. I had no way to make certain the others were asleep. If I'd had to make a guess, it would have been that none of us would get much sleep that night. But finally the walls themselves seemed to fall into a fitful doze, as if acknowledging that the future was set and there was nothing to be changed by keeping watch through the night.

I threw back my covers and slipped out of bed, dressing quickly in my oldest clothes, the ones that made me look the most like a boy. My ears strained against the silence, alert for even the slightest sound. But the house stayed peaceful all around me. Whispering a prayer of thanks, I gathered the few belongings I had decided to take and tied them into my winter cloak. It was not as warm as my father's because it had no fur lining. But it would have to do. I took my bow and quiver full of arrows and slung them across my shoulders.

I tiptoed to the kitchen, wrapped some food in a knapsack, and retrieved a water skin. I would not risk filling it here but would do so from the stream. Then I let myself out of the house and walked quickly to the stables. I did not look back. I feared that if I did, I would lose my nerve, in spite of all my resolve.

It was fortunate that my father's great stallion and I were well acquainted with each other. Otherwise, my plan would have been over even before it had started. I fed the horse a bit of apple, and he let me saddle him without protest. I was just leading him from the stall when the door to the stable slid open. I stopped dead in my tracks.

"I thought so," Min Xian said as she poked her head around the door.

"Min Xian," I breathed. "Be quiet. Come in and close the door."

"What's the point in doing that when you'll only open it right back up again?" she asked, but she did lower her voice. "You didn't think I was going to let you go without saying good-bye, did you?"

"You knew I would do this?" I asked, suddenly feeling the hot sting of tears behind my eyes.

"Of course I did, little one," my nurse said. She crossed to where I stood, my hand on the horse's neck, and she placed her hand on my arm. "I saw you watching them at dinner, and saw into your heart, my Mulan. I should stop you."

"No. You shouldn't," I said. "It's the only way. You know it too, Min Xian."

"I don't know that," she answered crossly. But I knew Min Xian too well to be deceived. The longer she sounded cross, the longer she could postpone crying.

"But even these old eyes can see that it may be the best way," Min Xian went on. "Now turn around. You can't go off with all that hair. It'll give you away for sure. If I cut it and then tie it back, you'll at least stand a chance of looking like other peasant boys."

"Oh, thank you, Min Xian," I said, for I had worried about my hair.

I turned my head and felt her strong fingers grasp my braid. A moment later there was a tug and a rasping sound as Min Xian moved the knife blade back and forth. And then my head felt strange and light. Min Xian tucked the thick braid of hair into her sash. Then she quickly rebraided what was left on my head, tying the end with a leather thong.

"That's better," she said. "Now take this." She turned me back around and thrust a bundle into my hands.

"I packed food," I protested.

Min Xian gave a grunt. "Take more. It's a two-day journey to the muster place, and you've never ridden as hard as you must to make it there in time. If you faint from hunger as soon as you arrive, you'll be no use to anyone."

"Only girls faint from hunger," I said. "And I'm no longer a girl, remember?"

Min Xian gave a snort. "Hold your tongue unless

you're spoken to," she said. "Go quickly. Don't stop to make friends on the road. It will be full of many such as you, going to do their duty."

She stepped back. "Get along with you now. And remember that no matter what you show on the outside, inside you have a tiger's heart."

"I will," I promised. "Please tell my father and Zao Xing that I love them."

Min Xian nodded. "I'll hardly need to do that," she said. "They already know it, and they'll feel it all the more strongly once you are gone. Hurry now. Before I change my mind and wake them up instead."

"Help me, then," I said. Together we carefully lifted each of the horse's hooves and wrapped them in cloth. This would keep the noise from giving us away as we crossed our courtyard. Once I reached the hard-packed earth of the road, I would take them off. There would no longer be a need for silence.

Min Xian went with me as far as our gate, helping me to ease it open. I led the horse through and stopped to free his feet. Min Xian took the cloths from me, clutching them to her chest.

"Mulan."

I swung myself up into the saddle, heart pounding. I was really going to do this. I was going off to war.

"What is it?" I asked. "Speak quickly, Min Xian."

"There is something you should know before you go," she said. "Something that I should have had the courage to tell you long ago."

"What is it?" I asked again.

"Your mother's name was Xiao Lizi."

Before I could answer, Min Xian stepped back through the gate and shut it fast behind her.

I put my heels to the horse's flanks, urging him out into the road. I was glad he was sure-footed, even in the dark, because I could see nothing through the tears that filled my eyes.

My mother's name was "Little Plum."

TWELVE

I arrived at the assembly place for the Son of Heaven's great army after two days of hard riding. Along the way I had plenty of opportunities to be grateful for Min Xian's advice. Two long days in the saddle is not the same as an afternoon's ride for pleasure. By the time I reached the place of muster, my whole body was aching and sore. But I had done it, becoming one of the steady stream of men and boys traveling to do their duty.

I moved as swiftly as I could, and I spoke to as few people as possible.

The longer I traveled, the colder it became, for I was moving almost due north. More than once I wished for my father's fur-lined cloak.

For as long as I live, I will never forget my first sight of the great encampment and the army that the Son of Heaven had called together to defend China. It was a large valley at the mouth of the mountain pass through which the emperor's spies had said the Huns planned to attack. As I approached, it seemed to me that the land itself had come alive, for it moved with men and horses. The air above it was filled with the smoke of cooking fires. A long line of recruits clogged the road that was the only access. As we waited, word of what was happening began to move down the line.

Each new recruit was being asked a series of questions before he was given his assignment and permitted to enter the valley. The army would be divided into three large companies, each one led by one of the princes.

"As for me, I hope to fight with Prince Jian," said the man beside me. He was not quite my father's age. Though, with his face lined from the sun it was difficult to tell.

"You'd do better to fight for the middle son, Prince Guang. He's the better fighter, or so they say," commented another.

"That may be," the first man answered. "But I've heard that General Yuwen is commanding Prince Jian's forces. He's an old campaigner. I've fought with him before. And the young prince is the emperor's favorite, or so they say."

"That must make things happy at home," a voice behind me remarked.

The older man beside me snorted. "I know nothing of court intrigues," he replied. "But I do know this: Many things can happen in the heat of battle."

After that there was no more talking, as each of us stayed busy with our own thoughts. Soon enough I came to the head of the line.

Where the road ended and the encampment

began, the land widened out. There a group of experienced soldiers were interviewing the recruits and handing out assignments. Those of us on horseback now dismounted. I reached to thread my fingers through the horse's mane, and he turned his head, blowing softly into my face through his large nostrils, as if to offer reassurance.

"You, boy, what is your name?" the official barked.

I had given this a lot of thought and had decided to stick to the truth as much as possible. I could hardly say my name was Hua Mulan, for there wasn't a boy on earth who was named orchid. But I thought that I might risk my family name.

"Hua Gong-shi," I answered as boldly as I could.

"Huh," the soldier said, and I bit the inside of my cheek to hold back a smile. He sounded exactly like my father.

"You are young to have such a fine horse," the soldier said. All of a sudden he thrust his face right into mine. "Unless, of course, you stole it."

"I am not a thief," I said, feeling my cheeks warm with the insult. My heart began to pound in fear and anger combined. But even then my mind was racing faster.

Think, Mulan, I told myself. If I could think, and act, quickly enough, perhaps I could turn this situation to my advantage.

"The horse was a gift," I said now. "From General Yuwen Huaji himself. Go and ask him, if you don't believe me."

The soldier made a sound of disgust. But he did step back. I had managed to sow a seed of doubt.

"You expect me to disturb a general on your behalf?" the soldier inquired, his tone sarcastic. "Perhaps I should just turn you over to his aide right here and now. He'll soon get to the bottom of this."

"Perhaps you should," I said at once.

"You," the soldier said, pointing to a boy even younger than I who stood nearby. "Go and get General Yuwen's aide and bring him back here. I can't remember his name, but the one who's always with him. You know the one."

"His name," I said firmly, "is Li Po."

"I can't believe it," Li Po said some time later. The fact that I had not stolen my remarkable horse had been established once and for all. I was now assigned to Prince Jian's forces—specifically, to an elite archer corps. I had Li Po to thank for both these things, just as I had him to thank for my first hot meal since leaving home.

"Which part?" I asked now.

"Any part," Li Po said as he handed me a cup of steaming tea. Though our conversation was impassioned, we were both careful to keep our voices low.

"When I realized it was you, I thought my heart would stop. You shouldn't be here. This is not a game, Mulan. What on earth were you thinking?" Li Po frowned. Before I could answer these questions, he posed another. "What did you say you were calling yourself?"

Cameron Dokey

"Hua Gong-shi," I answered, taking the tea from him just in time. At my reply Li Po dropped his head down into his hands, though not before I thought I saw his lips begin to curve into a reluctant smile.

"You told them your name was Bow-and-Arrow?"

"It was a better choice than Wood Orchid, don't you think?" I said.

Li Po sighed. "I am happy to see you. Don't misunderstand me," he said, lifting his head, "but . . ."

"My stepmother is going to have a baby," I said before he could go on. "The emperor sent no word to my father. Instead we received the same summons as everyone else—that every household in China must send a man to fight."

"Every household must send one *man*," Li Po said. "That's precisely my point."

"Tell me something, Li Po," I said. "How long do you think my father would have lasted as a foot soldier? What do you think it would do to him to ride away to war leaving yet another pregnant wife behind?"

Li Po's face looked pinched, as if he hated to speak his arguments aloud. "Your father is not the only older man to answer the emperor's call."

"You're absolutely right," I answered. "He is not. But I saw an opportunity to spare him, and I took it. It is done. Hua Gong-shi is not the only lad to answer the summons either. And I have skills many other *boys* do not. You ought to know that. You saw to it yourself."

"I'll have to tell General Yuwen. You realize that, don't you?" Li Po said. "He'll recognize the bow on your back, not to mention the horse."

"You must do what you think is best," I replied. "That's what I've done, and all your fine arguments will not make me sorry for it."

I sat back, and we eyed each other for a moment. "You look well, Li Po."

"Stop trying to flatter me," he said. "It won't get you anywhere, not for the rest of the day, anyhow. I'm going to stay mad at you for at least that long."

Without warning he leaned forward and pulled me into his arms. "If you die, I'm never going to forgive you, or myself. But I am glad to see you, Mulan."

"Gong-shi," I mumbled against his chest as I wrapped my own arms around him and held on tight. "I'm surprised the general trusts you if you can't remember even the simplest details."

Li Po gave a strangled laugh, and we released each other. It was just in time, for in the next moment the flap of the tent whipped back. General Yuwen stood in the opening.

"I heard we had an interesting new recruit," he said. He moved forward, letting the tent flap fall closed behind him.

I got to my feet, prepared to bow. "Stop that," the general said. He caught me to him, much as Li Po had, and then held me at arm's length while he studied me.

"I ought to take you out behind the tents and thrash you," he said.

I managed a shaky laugh. "You'll have to get in line behind Li Po."

"You should listen to her ... him," Li Po said, making an exasperated sound as he corrected himself. "I may not agree with everything your new recruit has to say, but he does make several interesting points."

"My stepmother is going to have a child," I told General Yuwen. "The emperor sent no word for my father, no call to return to his previous duties. It seems he is not to be forgiven, even now, when the wisdom of his words has been proved beyond a doubt."

General Yuwen nodded, his lips forming a thin line as if he were holding something bitter in his mouth.

"My father and stepmother, they love each other," I said softly, and suddenly my voice caught at the back of my throat. "You know what it is like to lose someone you love. You watched your own son die. Once I saw the way my father and stepmother felt about each other, I could not let him respond to the emperor's summons. *I could not.* So I took the horse and came in his place."

I gave a watery laugh. "And the funny thing is, I didn't even like her at first."

"Mulan," General Yuwen said gently. "Mulan."

Then, just as swiftly as the tears had come, they vanished. I was through with crying. I steadied my feet, put my hands on my hips, and lifted my chin, just as I had on a day that seemed a very long time ago. The day when I had knelt, soaking wet, in a stream and seen two men on horseback for the very first time.

"No," I said. "I am no longer Mulan. I stopped being Mulan two days ago. Take me out behind the tents and thrash me if you must, but you won't make me return home. I'm staying, whether you like it or not."

"She told them her name was Hua Gong-shi," Li Po spoke up. "So I assigned her to the prince's new corps of archers. She shoots almost as well as I do."

"I am well aware of that," General Yuwen said. "Did I not give her my own son's bow?" He passed a hand across his face, and for the first time I saw how tired he was. "Well," he said.

He moved farther into the tent and sat down. Li Po poured him a cup of tea.

"My heart may wish you safe at home, Mulan, but the heart is not always granted what it desires. This much all three of us know. Given the circumstances, I think Li Po's choice makes good sense. Now I will drink my tea, with no further discussion."

We all drank in silence for several moments.

"The prince has asked to meet you," General Yuwen finally said.

"To meet me?" I echoed, astonished. "Why?"

"He meets as many of his new recruits as he can. But he pays particular attention to his archers. He is a fine bowman himself. And then there was the . . . somewhat unusual manner of your arrival. Did you really think a boy leading a war horse was going to go unnoticed?"

"Apparently, I didn't think at all," I said.

Li Po gave a snort. "I could have told you that much."

"I told the one who questioned me that the horse was a gift from you," I said to General Yuwen.

"We will let the story stand," the general said, and nodded. "I have told the prince that you are a distant relation who once did my son a service, and that the bow you carry and the horse you ride were your rewards. I think he wonders at it, a little, but he hardly has the time to ask questions. There are many more important things to think about and do."

"What of the Huns?" I inquired.

"All in good time," General Yuwen replied. He got to his feet. "First I must take you to meet Prince Jian. After that I will take you to be with the rest of the archers. Li Po is their captain. Did he tell you that?"

"No," I said. "He was full of other information, but he left that out."

General Yuwen gave a quick smile. "I have decided it would be wise for my young relative to share Li Po's tent," he said. "So that he has someone to guide him during his first experience of war."

"Let us hope that it will also be the last," I said.

"We shall all hope that," said the general. "Now come. I will take you to Prince Jian."

Thirteen

"The truth is, you've arrived just in time," General Yuwen said as he walked beside me.

All around us men snapped to attention as the general strode by. Everywhere I looked it seemed to me that I saw men tending to equipment and horses. An uneasy alertness seemed to lie over men and animals alike, as if they understood that all too soon the battle would commence.

"Our scouts report that the Huns are closer than we thought. They will be here by the end of the week. How best to meet them has been the cause of much discussion."

"Oh, but surely . . ." I began. I'd been in camp less than an hour. It was hardly up to me to voice an opinion as to how the battle should be fought.

"No, tell me," General Yuwen said, as if he had read my thoughts. "You should hold your tongue before others but not before Li Po or me, at least not when we are alone."

"I thought the way to meet them had already been decided," I said. "The Huns must come through the mountain pass just beyond this valley or not at all."

"That is true enough," General Yuwen agreed, "but there is more. There is also a second, smaller pass less than a day's ride from here. It is so narrow no more than two men can ride abreast. Prince Jian thinks this pass should be protected as well."

"But his brothers do not agree?" I asked.

"Not entirely, no. Prince Ying is cautious to express his opinions. That is his way. But Prince Guang has openly ridiculed his younger brother. We may be far from the imperial palace, but court intrigue is still very much with us, I'm sorry to say. And that is a thing of which Prince Guang is a master."

"There," General Yuwen said, pointing. "Those are the princes' tents. The one flying the green banner is Prince Jian's."

The princes' tents stood in the very center of the camp, arranged so that they formed a great triangle. Each had a pennant of a different color flying from its center roof pole. The red designated the eldest, Prince Ying, General Yuwen told me, and the blue the middle brother, Prince Guang. Each banner displayed the same symbol, the mark of the princes: the figure of a dragon with four claws. Only the emperor could display the figure of the powerful five-clawed dragon. Even from a distance I could hear the sound the banners made as they snapped in the cold afternoon wind.

I was curious to see Prince Jian, the young man whose life my father had once saved, and whose fate was so closely tied to that of all China. *Was it a blessing or a curse to bear the weight of such a prophecy?* I wondered.

"What is he like?" I inquired.

"Prince Jian?" General Yuwen asked.

I nodded.

"He is unlike anyone else I have ever met," the general said honestly. "Of course he pays attention to protocol. He is a prince. But he is also . . . approachable. The common soldiers love him, because he lets them speak."

"And his brothers?"

"Prince Ying is the oldest, as you know," General Yuwen said. "He has many talents. But I think that sometimes Prince Ying is misunderstood—especially by his father. The prince is a scholar, not a soldier. He has a deep and subtle mind. He will make a great statesman someday, a great emperor during peacetime."

"And the middle son, Prince Guang?"

"He is the one to watch with both eyes open," General Yuwen replied. "He is a courtier through and through. To turn your back on him is to risk exposing it to a knife. He resents being the second son very much, I think."

"Is it true what the men say? That the emperor favors Prince Jian?"

"It is not my place," the general answered, "to claim to know what is in the Son of Heaven's heart." He glanced over at me. "But to speak my own mind . . . I believe the emperor does favor Jian over the others, and that they all suffer as a result. To promote the youngest over the eldest disrupts the proper order of things. Only strife can come of it.

"Besides, I do not believe that Prince Jian seeks out his father's special favor. Though, like all dutiful sons, he desires his love."

"What does Prince Jian want, then?" I asked.

"To be allowed to be himself more than anything, I think," General Yuwen answered, his tone thoughtful. "Not an easy task for a prince. But even more than that, I believe Prince Jian wants what is best for China."

"Determining what that is cannot be an easy thing either, I should think," I observed, remembering my father.

General Yuwen gave a short bark of laughter. "And I think you are right."

We reached the princes' tents. A sentry snapped to attention at our approach. The general announced that we had come at Prince Jian's request, and the sentry gestured to one of the guards stationed on either side of the prince's tent flap. The flap was closed to keep out the cold and to provide privacy. The guard ducked inside to inform the prince of our arrival.

"No more talking," General Yuwen said in a low voice. "But remember what I have spoken. Use your ears, not your tongue, and keep your eyes open."

"I will," I promised.

The guard reappeared and gestured us forward. The prince's tent was much larger than General

Yuwen's, as befitted his rank. There were tables for maps, and chairs for the prince and his advisers. Rich rugs covered the hard-packed earth of the tent floor. General Yuwen and I entered and made our obeisance, kneeling and pressing our foreheads to the ground.

"Ah, Huaji," I heard a voice above my head say. "There you are. So this is the lad whose name is Bow-and-Arrow. Stand up, both of you. I would like to take a look at you, boy."

I got to my feet, though I was careful to keep my eyes lowered. My heart was pounding so loud it seemed to me all those in the tent must be able to hear it.

"Let me see your face," instructed Prince Jian.

Gong-shi. My name is Gong-shi, I told myself over and over. But Gong-shi was like Mulan in one important respect. Like her, he possessed the heart of a tiger.

I lifted my head and gazed directly into Prince Jian's eyes.

They were dark, like my own. Glittering like onyx beads, they narrowed ever so slightly as he studied me.

Those eyes will not miss much, I thought.

Prince Jian's face was striking. Taken feature by feature, I could not have described it as a handsome one. His forehead was, perhaps, too high and wide, his chin too strong. And even though at that moment I thought I detected the hint of a smile, if I'd had to make a guess, it would have been that all too often and particularly of late his mouth had been pressed into a thin, determined line.

But, taken all together, it was a face that commanded attention. Prince Jian had a face that, once seen, would be hard to look away from, a face that would inspire others to fight for his cause.

Though his clothing was made of rich fabrics, the prince was as simply dressed as I was. His clothing was practical, ready for action. This fit with the man General Yuwen had described, one who did not stand on ceremony. A man who commanded respect not just because of what he was, but because of *who* he was.

And I found myself wondering, as if from out of nowhere, what it would take to make him truly smile.

"You are very young, are you not?" the prince asked softly. During the moments in which I had been studying his face, he had been making just as thorough a perusal of mine. I dropped to one knee, once more looking at the ground.

"I am old enough to dedicate myself to your service, and to that of China, sire," I replied. It was true that I had promised General Yuwen that I would use my ears and eyes rather than my tongue. But the prince's question called for a response.

You are not all that much older than I am, I thought, even as I focused my eyes on the rich carpets.

It had been my father's rescue of this prince that

had earned him the right to marry my mother. Both events had occurred when Prince Jian was not yet ten years old. He would be in his early twenties now.

"That is well spoken," Prince Jian remarked, "but it will take more than fine words to defeat the Huns."

He stepped away, and I felt my heart beat a little easier. I had not offended him by speaking, after all.

"That is your son's bow he carries, is it not?" the prince continued, addressing General Yuwen now.

"It is, my lord."

"An interesting present. Though I am sure you would have bestowed such a gift only on one who was worthy," Prince Jian remarked.

"I am utterly unworthy, sire," I said, and then bit my tongue. For now I *had* spoken out of turn, since the prince had not been speaking to me at all. "I can only seek to repay General Yuwen's generosity by proving my worthiness by fighting in China's cause."

"Well spoken once more," the prince replied. "What do you think, Huaji? This one has a monkey's tongue. I'm beginning to think there is more to him than meets the eye."

You have no idea, I thought, grateful that protocol allowed me to keep my eyes upon the floor. I feared that if I looked at Prince Jian, I would give myself away. There was something about him that seemed to draw the truth from those around him. I wondered what he would think if he knew the truth about me.

"I am tired of being inside," the prince suddenly

announced. "I've been in one tent or another poring over maps and arguing with my brothers since early this morning. I could use a little target practice myself, and I would like to see you shoot, boy. Let us go out, before the light fades."

"It shall be as it pleases Your Highness," I said.

The prince's boots came into my view, and then he briefly rested the fingers of one hand on the top of my bowed head.

"I doubt that very much," he said softly, "but let us see what a little target practice can do to improve my mood."

With the prince leading the way, we went outside.

Word spread quickly through the camp that Prince Jian intended to match shots with the youngest and newest member of his elite corps of archers. By the time we arrived at the target range, a large crowd had already gathered. All the soldiers fell to their knees at Prince Jian's approach, but neither their presence nor the way they paid him honor seemed to improve the prince's mood. He made a curt gesture to General Yuwen, who commanded the men to stand up.

It might have been easy for the prince to ignore the crowd. He was royalty, after all, and had grown up amid the bustle of a palace. As for me, the crowd at the target range seemed enormous. And the army of which I was now a part constituted more people than I'd seen assembled in one place in my entire life. As I thought of all of these people who would be watching my every move, I felt a hard fist of fear form in the pit of my stomach.

"I will set Your Highness's arrows, if I may," General Yuwen offered as we approached the line from which we would shoot. A series of straw targets had been set up some distance away. With a jolt I saw that they were in the shapes of men.

Of course they are, I thought. *That is why we are all here, Mulan. To protect China, at our enemies' cost.*

Though the targets I now faced were larger than any Li Po and I had practiced on, I still wondered whether or not I would be able to hit one, for I had never shot at anything like this before. *But that is what you will be doing*, I thought. *Soon enough.* And when it came time to aim then, it would not be at men of straw but at men of flesh and blood. I fought down a sudden wave of dizziness.

"I accept your offer, Huaji," replied Prince Jian. "Three arrows, I think, to start. That should be enough to see what this small one is made of, don't you think?"

And then, without warning, Prince Jian smiled. It lit up his features, making the spirit within him blaze forth. Prince Jian clearly enjoyed a challenge.

With this realization I felt the fist in my stomach relax just a little. While there were many differences between us, in this the prince and I were exactly alike. I, too, loved a challenge, so much so that I had yet to find one that could make me back down. I was not about to start today, no matter how out of my league I felt.

Very well, Highness, I thought. *Let us see what an unknown archer and a prince may do, side by side.*

"And Gong-shi?" the prince asked. "What of him?"

"I will aid him, with your permission," said a voice I recognized.

"Ah, Li Po," Prince Jian said with a nod. "That is well. What do you say? Shall we give Gong-shi one shot extra, to let him test the wind?"

"No, Highness." I spoke before Li Po could reply. A sudden hush fell over the crowd. In it I realized that perhaps the words "no" and "Highness" did not belong together, at least not in a statement by themselves.

"With respect," I blundered on. "You have shaped your targets like the enemies of China, and they will show me no such kindness."

Again I felt Prince Jian's keen eyes roam my face. "The lad makes a good point," he acknowledged, lifting up his voice. "It shall be as he says." And now the silence of the crowd was broken by murmurs of astonishment or respect, I could not tell.

Concentrating fiercely, trying to shut out all but the task at hand, I took the quiver from around my neck and handed it to Li Po. General Yuwen was already in possession of Prince Jian's arrows. The prince and I took our positions, sighting toward one of the targets. Behind us Li Po and General Yuwen knelt and thrust two arrows each, points first, into the cold ground.

Without looking back Prince Jian extended a hand. General Yuwen placed an arrow into the flat of his palm. The prince wasted no time. With swift, sure motions he set his arrow to the bow, pulled back the string, and let the arrow fly.

Straight and true toward the target it went, embedding itself not in the straw man's chest but through its throat. A cheer went up from the soldiers, even as I felt my body tingle in shock.

I might not have thought of that, I realized. If I had shot first, chances were good I would have aimed for the target's heart. But a true warrior would be wearing armor. Though a common soldier might not, his body would be protected. This was why Prince Jian had shot through the neck. It was one of the few unprotected places on a warrior's body.

I swallowed, feeling my throat constrict. It seemed to me that I could feel the gaze of every single eye in the crowd. The bow, which I had so carefully and proudly trained myself to use, felt heavy and awkward in my hands. If I failed, I would be a laughingstock. And worse, my failure could reflect on Prince Jian.

I extended my arm back, as the prince had done.

"Remember to plant your feet," Li Po murmured for my ears alone as he placed the shaft of the arrow into my palm. "Remember to breathe. Above all, remember who you are, for there is no one like you in all China, not even the royal prince who stands at your side."

At his words I felt my fear pass away. I returned to my true self. It did not matter that I now was called by a boy's name. Even Prince Jian ceased to be important. All that was important was that in my heart I knew what I could do. I knew who I was.

I was the only child of the great general Hua Wei. I had come here so that he might have a long and happy life, and to give him a gift he had not asked for, that of holding his second child on the day that child was born.

I had come because, as strange and unusual as I was, I thought I could accomplish one unusual feat more. One that had been inside my heart from the moment it had begun to beat, or so it seemed to me in that moment. I had come to make my father as proud of me, his daughter, as he would have been of any son.

Or, barring any of these fine things, I wished, quite profoundly, that I might not make a complete and utter fool of myself.

I widened my stance and pulled back on the bow. I sighted along the shaft of the arrow, picturing in my mind where I wished it to go. The cold evening breeze tugged at my sleeves, as if urging me to let go. But I did not listen. For once in my life I remembered to be patient.

The wind died away, and I let the arrow fly.

My shot was not as perfect as Prince Jian's. His had pierced the target straight through the middle of its throat, while mine passed through just to the right.

But it was a good shot nevertheless. A killing shot, had that distant figure been alive. As my arrow found its mark, a second cheer went up.

"The boy can shoot. Perhaps he's got the right name after all," I heard one of the soldiers remark.

"Move the targets back," Prince Jian commanded. Once again he flashed me that smile. "And turn them to the side." A man in profile offered less of a target than one facing front.

"And my young friend here will shoot first this time."

Taking this second shot was more difficult than the first. One good shot can be made by even the worst of archers. And this time I let my nervousness get the best of me, my arrow passing not through the target's neck but embedding itself in the target's upper arm.

"The shot is still a good one," the prince said over the murmur of the crowd. "For now that arm is useless and cannot be raised against China."

He accepted an arrow from General Yuwen and let it fly. Like the first, the prince's second arrow passed cleanly through the target's neck, piercing it from side to side. Again a cheer went up from the crowd. Then it was cut off abruptly as, with one body, the assembled spectators dropped to their knees.

"Entertaining the troops, I see," remarked an unfamiliar voice.

Belatedly I knelt myself, with Li Po at my side.

Even General Yuwen and Prince Jian made obeisance,
though the prince merely bowed.

"So this is the boy who carries a warrior's bow," the
voice went on. "I hope you can do more than just carry
it on your back."

I could not have answered, even if I'd thought a
response was necessary. My tongue seemed glued to
the roof of my mouth.

"How many shots?"

"Three, Brother," Prince Jian said. "Two are accomplished. There is one to go."

"Why not shoot together?" the newcomer asked.
"Prince and commoner, standing side by side. Such an
inspiration, wouldn't you agree?"

This must be Prince Guang, I realized. Though
surely he would never have performed the act he was
urging on Prince Jian. For if a prince and commoner
performed the same action but only the commoner
prevailed . . .

Oh, be careful, I thought. Then I wondered if I was
cautioning myself or Prince Jian.

"An excellent suggestion," Prince Jian answered. "For
surely we all carry the same desire in our hearts to rid
China of her enemies, prince and commoner alike."

"Get up, boy," Prince Guang instructed in a curt
tone. I stood, praying that my trembling legs would
hold me up, and was careful to keep my face lowered.
With a gloved hand Prince Guang grasped my chin
and forced my face upward.

"This one has a soft face, like a girl's," he scoffed.

His words made my blood run cold even as it rushed to my face. Though, in truth, I did not think Prince Guang had the slightest idea that he'd guessed my secret. He was simply looking to add further insult to his younger brother, should I outshoot him.

Prince Guang released my chin and stepped away, wiping his hand against his overcoat as if the touch of my skin had soiled the leather of his glove.

"I look forward to the contest."

At a signal from Prince Jian the final target was moved into position and placed so that it was an equal distance between us both. The prince held out a hand for his arrow and nodded to me to do the same.

"Listen to me, Gong-shi," he said so quietly that I thought his voice carried no farther than General Yuwen and Li Po standing directly behind us.

"Nothing is more important than defeating the enemies of China. When you let your arrow fly, remember that."

"Sire, I will," I promised.

Together we took our positions, sighting the target. As I looked down the shaft of my arrow, the world dropped away. I did not feel the tension of the crowd or Prince Guang's clever malice. There was only the feel of the bow and arrow in my hands, the tug of wind, the sight of the target. A great stillness seemed to settle over me. The whole world seemed sharp and clear and calm. I pulled in a single breath and held it.

Prince Jian is right, I thought. *Nothing is more important than defeating the enemies of China.*

135

I released the breath, and with it the arrow. For better or worse, the deed was done.

I was barely aware of Prince Jian beside me, mirroring my actions. The arrows flew so quickly that I could hardly mark their flights with my eyes. As if from a great remove I heard the sounds they made as they struck home. For several seconds not a single person reacted. And now the only sound that I could hear was that of my own thundering heart.

Then, suddenly, it did not beat alone.

For it seemed to me that I could hear a second heartbeat, pounding out a rhythm a perfect match to my own. Its beat had been there all the time, I realized, shoring mine up, urging it on.

Prince Jian, I thought.

Then every other thought was driven from me as the crowd of soldiers surrounding me and the prince erupted in a great roar of sound.

Now, at last, I realized what my eyes had been trying to tell me all this time. The prince's arrow and my own had found precisely the same mark, passing directly through the target's throat. It was the best shot I had ever made, and I had done it with my heart beating in time to that of Prince Jian.

He moved to stand beside me then, clapping me on the back as he threw back his head and laughed in delight. I staggered a little under the gesture, for, abruptly, I was dizzy.

"Well done," Prince Jian said, his hand resting on my shoulder. "You come by your name honestly,

Gong-shi, and I think you are more than worthy of that bow.

"Bring me the arrows," he instructed Li Po.

Li Po took off running, returning a moment later with the arrows in both hands. At a nod from Prince Jian, Li Po held the arrows up for all to see.

The points were joined. Prince Jian and I had each shot so true that the points of our arrows had pierced each other and the target both.

"That is fine shooting," I heard the voice I knew was Prince Guang's say. I would have knelt, but for the sudden tightening of Prince Jian's grip on my shoulder. I stood still but trained my eyes on the rough stubble of grass that covered the ground of the target range.

"I will remember it, and you, Little Archer."

Without another word Prince Guang turned and walked away. I swayed, my legs threatening to give out under me. I thought I heard Prince Jian murmur something beneath his breath.

"This lad is ready to drop, Huaji," he said to General Yuwen. "Where do you lodge him?"

"With Li Po," General Yuwen said.

"Good." Prince Jian nodded. "Have Li Po get him something to eat, and then let him rest. But have Gong-shi at the ready, in case I should call."

Prince Jian gave my shoulder one last squeeze and let me go. "You have keen eyes and a strong heart, Little Archer," he said before he turned away. "I have need of both. I will not forget you either."

Fourteen

"I wish they'd stop staring," I murmured to Li Po as we crossed the camp the next morning.

I had gotten my first full night's sleep since leaving home, and had enjoyed the first hot breakfast, besides. Though General Yuwen had stayed with him long into the night, Prince Jian had not sent for Li Po or me after all. But shortly after breakfast we received word that the last of the scouts had returned. Now a meeting was being held in Prince Ying's tent, and we had been summoned. General Yuwen was already there.

"You'd do well to get used to it," Li Po replied. "You are famous." He glanced down, mischief briefly dancing in his eyes. "Little Archer."

I made a face. If we'd been alone, I'd have stuck out my tongue. But I knew better than to do that when the entire camp seemed to have their eyes on me, watching to see what impossible deed I'd perform next.

"And I wish they'd stop that, too," I said.

At this Li Po grinned outright. "I know. But you can't really blame them, any of them. You *are* famous now, and you *aren't* very tall, not for a boy."

"Especially not after you've done your best to whittle me down to size," I remarked. We walked in silence for several moments. "Why should the princes summon us to this council?"

"I am included because I am the captain of Prince Jian's archers," Li Po answered. "You, because he has asked for you, I suppose."

"Prince Guang will be there too, won't he?"

Li Po nodded. "It's a pity that he seems to have taken a dislike to you. Prince Guang is not a good adversary to have."

We walked in silence for a moment while I digested this fact.

"Why should he bother with me at all?" I asked finally. "I'm only a common boy. Surely I'm not worth his time."

"Under ordinary circumstances, I'd say you were right," Li Po replied. "But our present situation is far from ordinary." He turned his head to look at me. "You really *did* make an extraordinary shot yesterday, you know."

I had told no one what had happened in the moments after I'd let my final arrow fly, not even Li Po. I wasn't certain that he would understand. I wasn't all that sure I did myself. I was closer to Li Po than to anyone else, but never had I felt as close to another human being as I had when I'd felt my heart beat in time to that of Prince Jian. It was as if we had become the same person, our two hearts beating as one.

"It's not only your shooting, of course," Li Po went on. I recalled my wandering thoughts. "There's also the fact that Prince Jian has taken a liking to you. That alone would be enough to bring you to both his brothers' attention."

"Let's hope the oldest, Prince Ying, doesn't decide to dislike me on sight too," I remarked.

"That is not his way," Li Po replied. "But if you will listen to some advice . . ."

I nodded my head, to show I would, and Li Po continued.

"It might be a good idea for you to do a little noticing of your own. General Yuwen says you can tell much about a man by studying those whose company he chooses. It's always a good idea to know who the favorites are."

"That is good advice," I said, and nodded.

"As long as you don't let anyone see that you are watching," Li Po added after a moment. "The trick is—"

"I know what the trick is," I interrupted, struggling to push back a sudden surge of annoyance. "The trick is to watch without looking like you're doing it. What makes you so bossy all of a sudden? All of this is new to me, I admit, but I'm not completely without brains, you know."

Li Po stopped walking and seized me by one arm.

"If I'm bossy, it's because I'm worried about you," he said, speaking in a low, intense voice. "Is that so wrong? In a matter of days target practice will be over and we will all be going to war. And you are not like other people. You are unpredictable. You always have been, Mulan. If I'm warning you, it's only for your own good."

"My name is Gong-shi," I corrected. "And since when are you always careful and wise?"

Li Po gave my arm a shake. "That is not the point."

"Then, what is?" I cried.

"The point," Li Po said through clenched teeth. "The point is that I don't want you to die. I don't want to ride home and have to explain to your father why I didn't take one look at you and send you right back home where you belong. It's what I should have done. I never should have let things come this far."

"You didn't have a choice," I answered. "And neither did I. Not once Prince Jian asked me to shoot at his side. Before that, even, when the guard accused me of stealing my father's horse. It's done. Let it go, Li Po. I can't change things and neither can you.

"Besides, we went over this yesterday, when I first arrived. Let us not spend the hours we have together arguing like children."

Li Po let go of my arm. "You're right," he said, his voice still strained. "I know you're right. But I can't help but feel afraid for us both. When this is over, I still plan to shake you until your teeth rattle."

"Yesterday it was thrashing me behind the tents. Today it's shaking me until my teeth rattle," I said. "Make up your mind."

"I'm giving serious consideration to both," Li Po said, but now I heard a hint of laughter in his tone.

"Well," I answered, "at least you'll have a while to make up your mind. Any thrashing you mete out will have to wait until after we've defeated the Huns. Now come on. Let's go."

We walked in silence the rest of the way. Arriving at Prince Ying's tent, we identified ourselves to the guards outside. A moment later General Yuwen appeared in the flap opening.

"Good. You are here," he said. "Come inside, but do so quietly, and keep your wits about you."

We ducked inside the tent. General Yuwen made a gesture, showing us our places. The center of the room was dominated by several tables filled with charts and maps. The princes and their advisers were bent over them, talking quietly. Servants and lesser soldiers stood along the perimeter. Li Po and I took our place among them. I was glad that Li Po had warned me about what to expect, though I still had to struggle to control my surprise.

Everyone—even the servants—was standing up.

It was Prince Jian's doing, Li Po had explained. The prince had made his position clear at the very first council of war and had refused to back down. He would not discuss battle strategy with men on their knees. A man should be able to stand on his own two feet when deciding the best way to send others into battle—when weighing the options on which his own life might hang, and the lives of his soldiers.

But Prince Jian had not stopped with insisting the generals be allowed to stand in his presence. He insisted the soldiers called to the councils should be allowed to do so as well, for it was their fate that was under discussion. It was an unheard-of change in protocol. Prince Guang had been furious, but Prince Jian had not budged. He would not ask any man to kneel before him when they were both doing the same thing: trying to determine the best way to safeguard China.

Prince Ying had agreed to his brother's terms first. Prince Guang had held out longer. But word of Prince Jian's actions had spread quickly through the camp. His popularity had skyrocketed. It was said that even those soldiers not directly assigned to Prince Jian's service would willingly die for him. For he treated them not like pieces on a game board but like men. In the end Prince Guang had given in.

The result was that all those who would plan strategy with the princes were allowed to move around the room as they wished, though I soon noted how careful everyone was to keep a respectful distance from the princes. But even this much freedom was a drastic change from years of tradition.

Like me, it seemed that Prince Jian was different.

"You still insist on ignoring the smaller pass," he was saying now, his tone heated. It seemed that Li Po and I had arrived in the midst of an argument.

"And you still insist on wasting resources where there is no danger," Prince Guang shot right back.

I let my eyes flicker to Prince Guang's face before returning to the spot on the wall of the tent I had chosen as my focus point. I had selected this spot with care, in an attempt to follow Li Po's instructions to keep my eyes open without appearing to do so. By choosing a spot about midway up the side of the tent opposite where I stood, I could see anyone in the room simply by shifting my eyes.

Prince Guang was the most handsome man that I had ever seen, a fact I had not been able to appreciate the day before. But it was not a kind of good looks that I found compelling. Instead the prince's smooth features made the gooseflesh rise along my arms. Prince Guang possessed the cold, smooth beauty of a snake.

This one loves himself more than he loves anything else around him, I thought. I wondered if that included China.

"It is not a waste of resources to protect China," Prince Jian began.

"Oh, spare me your sanctimonious proclamations about China," Prince Guang interrupted. "We all know about the prophecies and how important they make you, little brother. Perhaps you feel you are too important to fight. That is why you insist on guarding something that needs no protection."

"Enough!" the oldest brother, Prince Ying, cried. "You bicker like children, and it solves nothing."

It was the first time that he had spoken since Li Po and I had arrived. Following Prince Ying's outburst, a humming silence filled the tent. In it I could hear the dragon banner snapping in the wind high above me. I snuck a second look, at Prince Ying this time.

The Son of Heaven's firstborn was not as compelling as his brothers. He was not obviously handsome like Prince Guang. Nor did his features command a second look, as Prince Jian's did. But he was finely made, his voice and expression both more than a little stern. There was a crease permanently etched between his brows, as if from long hours of studying.

I remembered what General Yuwen had said, that Prince Ying possessed a fine and subtle mind. I wondered if it could maneuver through the rivalry between his brothers.

"We have been circling this matter for days," Prince Ying went on. "Both of you make good points." He frowned at Prince Guang. "Therefore, there is no need to cast doubts on anyone's honor. Just as there is no question of Jian leading an expedition to the smaller pass himself, assuming we decide to mount one. He is needed here, as we all are."

I half expected one or the other of the younger brothers to protest Prince Ying's words, but both stayed silent.

They respect him, then, I thought.

"Whose scouts were the last to return?" Prince Ying asked now.

"If it pleases Your Highness," said a voice I did not know, "those belonging to Prince Guang."

"And what do they tell us?" Prince Ying asked.

"The same thing all the other scouts have." Prince Guang spoke for himself this time. "That the Hun army is fast approaching, but there is nothing to show that they intend to divide their forces. They have no reason to. The second pass is simply too small."

"But you cannot *know* that," Prince Jian said, his voice impassioned. Almost against my will my eyes moved toward the sound of his voice. As he made his case, the color in his face was high. His dark eyes sparkled.

"We cannot afford to leave the smaller pass unguarded. Even a small force coming through it could do damage. It could attack the forces we have here from behind, or, even worse, the enemy could sweep on, into China."

He stepped to the table, stabbing a finger onto the map. "We have concentrated the majority of our forces here, in this valley, at *your* insistence, Brother."

His eyes were on Prince Guang as he spoke. "Only a small contingent of men remains to protect our father and Chang'an."

"We all agreed this valley was the clear choice," Prince Guang replied, his voice stiff.

"It *is* the clear choice," Prince Ying agreed. "Make your point, Jian."

"My point is that the Huns are not stupid," Prince Jian exclaimed. "And we should stop pretending that they are."

Once again he stabbed a finger against the map. "If we leave that pass unguarded, we leave China unprotected. A small force coming through it could ride unchallenged to Chang'an."

"Who do you propose we send to protect it?" Prince Ying asked. "Surely we need every man here. We cannot afford to divide our forces."

I know! I thought.

It was only as absolute silence filled the tent that I realized I had done the unthinkable: I had spoken aloud.

You are in for it now, Gong-shi, I thought.

Prince Guang was the first to recover.

"If it isn't the Little Archer," he said, his voice as cold and as smooth as a lacquer bowl. "Don't be afraid. Come forward, boy. Tell us what great plan you have devised in just one morning that the great generals of China have been unable to find after days of discussion."

"Guang, enough," Prince Ying said, his own tone mild. "You'll give the boy a heart attack. He already looks half-dead from fright."

"I beg Your Excellencies' pardons," I said, and now I did kneel, pressing my forehead to the ground. "I am presumptuous. I did not mean to speak aloud."

"But speak you did," Prince Ying replied. "And I agree with my brother, at least in part. Such an exclamation must have come straight from the heart. I would like to know what you think you've figured out."

"Stand up and speak, Gong-shi," Prince Jian instructed. "My brothers sound ferocious, but not even Guang will bite you."

I wouldn't be too sure about that, I thought.

Slowly I got to my feet. I could see General Yuwen standing just behind Prince Jian. Carefully I avoided his eyes.

"Now, then," Prince Jian said when I had risen. "What is so clear to you that the rest of us have failed to notice?"

"I do not claim that you have failed to notice it," I said, choosing my words with great care. "Only that I have not heard anyone speak of it this morning. But if the pass is truly so narrow that only two may ride abreast . . ."

All of a sudden Prince Jian laughed. "I think I see where he is going," he said. He shook his head ruefully, as if chastising himself. "The truth is, I should have thought of it."

"What?" Prince Guang barked, the single syllable like the crack of a whip.

Prince Jian turned to face his middle brother, a smile still lingering on his face.

"Archers."

By the time the hour for the midday meal arrived, the plan was in place. Rather than sending troops to try to block the pass, Prince Jian would send a division of his corps of archers. We would be accompanied by a small company of foot soldiers and several of the prince's swiftest runners. If the Huns did come through the pass, the archers and soldiers would hold them off. The runners would alert the main body of the army that reinforcements were needed. In this way a larger force would not be dispatched until the need had been proved beyond a doubt.

Nevertheless, it was a dangerous assignment. The Chinese force would be a small one, because although Prince Jian's brothers had finally agreed that such a force was necessary, they would agree to no more. We would have no experienced general to lead us. Instead that duty would fall upon Li Po as captain of the archers.

"Let those whom you send be volunteers," General Yuwen proposed. "For men will face even the greatest danger bravely if they choose it for themselves."

"That is a sound suggestion," Prince Ying agreed. "And, save for Jian's archers, let the men come from all our forces. Let anyone who wishes to volunteer be given permission to go. That way all will know there is no hidden favoritism. All have equal value."

"Be careful," Prince Guang warned. "You're starting to sound just like our unconventional younger brother. Father may not be pleased."

"Father is not here," Prince Ying replied, his voice calm. "A prince may have a costlier funeral, but his bones rot at the same rate as anyone else's. You might do well to remember that, Guang."

Prince Guang's face was suddenly suffused with color. "Is that a threat?" he demanded, stepping forward.

"Don't be ridiculous," Prince Jian said mildly. But I noticed that as he spoke he moved to place himself between his two brothers. "Ying simply reminds you of an obvious fact. In death, all men are alike."

The color still high in his face, Prince Guang pivoted on one heel, snapped his fingers for his advisers and attendants to follow, and strode from the tent. It seemed the council of war was over. Prince Jian had won the day, but not by much.

As soon as Prince Guang departed, Prince Jian came toward me.

"Highness, forgive me," I said, falling to my knees as he approached.

"No," he said simply. "I will not. You have helped to provide the solution to a problem that has troubled me for many days now. I am in your debt."

He reached down and placed a hand on my shoulder to urge me to my feet.

"Highness, if I may," Li Po spoke.

The prince nodded. "What is it, Li Po?"

"Perhaps Gong-shi should lead the archers," Li Po said. "Though he is young, the other men admire and respect him. I believe that they would follow him, even into great danger."

"No!" I cried out, appalled. "I am not experienced enough, and I . . ." I swallowed past a sudden lump in my throat. "I am not sure that I wish to command others."

"One cannot always choose whether to command or not," Prince Jian observed quietly. He reached to grip Li Po's shoulder. "Your suggestion does you credit, and I think I understand why you make it.

Even I have heard the men murmur of the young archer whose aim is as true as a prince. But I think I will leave things as they are, Li Po. Gong-shi makes a good point too. Your own experience will be needed."

"It shall be as you wish," Li Po vowed.

"Good," the prince said. "Then make ready, for you will go first thing in the morning. The Huns are close, and I do not like surprises."

He turned away. Together Li Po and I left Prince Ying's tent and made our way to our own in silence. This time I did not notice the stares as we walked through the camp. I was too busy wondering how Prince Jian would react if he knew the greatest surprise of all.

How would he feel if he learned that the archer who had fulfilled his desire to leave no portion of China unprotected was not a young lad named Gong-shi but a girl named Mulan?

FIFTEEN

I did not see Prince Jian for the rest of that day. Both Li Po and I were busy making preparations for our departure. After some discussion between Li Po and General Yuwen, it had been decided that half of our company of archers would go to the narrow pass.

"I would send all of you if I thought I could," General Yuwen said as we took our evening meal of rice and seasoned meat. He could have too, for every single member of the archer corps had volunteered to go. But a consultation between General Yuwen and his fellow commanders had determined that no more than half of the archers could be spared. The men had drawn lots to see who would accompany Li Po and me and who would remain with the main army.

"Do not wait, but send your runners as soon as you can if you need reinforcements," General Yuwen continued his instructions. "Once you have spent your arrows, you'll be down to hand-to-hand fighting, and if it comes to that, even a small force of Huns may overpower you."

"It shall be as you say," said Li Po.

General Yuwen sighed. "I wish your father were

here, Mulan," he said. "It would be good to fight once more with my old friend at my side."

"You do him honor," I said. "And I will do my best to do the same."

"Well," General Yuwen said. He stood up. "I have a final meeting with the other generals, and then to bed. Make sure to get a good night's sleep. There is no telling when the next one will be."

With that, he left the tent.

"I am going to bid the horse good night," I said. "Do you want to come?"

"I think I will stay here," Li Po answered. "I want to write a letter to my parents."

"I should have thought of that," I said as an image of my father and Zao Xing rose in my mind.

"I will write something for you, if you wish," Li Po offered.

"Thank you. I would like that," I replied.

All of a sudden Li Po grinned. "I could say hello to my mother for you," he said. "I could tell her she missed having a hero for a daughter-in-law."

"I'm sure she'd be delighted to hear the news," I answered with a chuckle, even as I felt my heart give a funny little squeeze inside my chest. "But I am not a hero."

"You mean, not yet," said Li Po.

I left our tent and made my way to the far edge of camp, where the horses were picketed all together. Dark came early at this time of year. The campfires were already lit.

The mood is different tonight, I thought. There was no raucous conversation. Instead all around me men were quietly and seriously attending to their tasks. Soon the true test of all our courage would come.

My father's horse was pleased to see me, particularly when I shared the carrot I had brought along. Even the horses seemed to sense that something was different. My father's stallion tossed his head and pawed the ground, as if eager to set off for the pass.

"Do not be impatient," I whispered against his dark, smooth neck. "The morning will come soon enough." It was only as I began to step away from the horse that I realized I was not alone. A figure stood in the shadows at the edge of camp, in the place where the light of the campfires did not quite reach. I gave a gasp, and the figure stepped forward.

It was Prince Jian.

"I did not mean to startle you—" he began, but he interrupted himself. "No, don't *do* that," he exclaimed as I began to kneel down. To my astonishment Prince Jian reached out and hauled me upright.

"I get so tired of staring at the tops of people's heads all day long. Stand up."

"It shall be—"

"Yes, yes," Prince Jian said impatiently. "I know. It shall be as My Highness wishes. Shall I tell you what I wish? Sometimes I wish I were not a prince at all."

"You should not say so!" I exclaimed, shocked and surprised. "If the men heard you, they would lose heart. They do not fight simply for China. They fight for you, because they love you."

As I do, I realized suddenly. And not just as a comrade in arms but as a soul mate. I could feel how Prince Jian's heart was made differently from all others, just as my own was. It wanted different things, things it didn't always know how to explain to itself. In this way it called out to mine.

But this was a secret my heart had to keep forever. For my heart was not just Gong-shi's. It was also Mulan's.

"I know the men love me," Prince Jian answered simply. "I know it. But sometimes I think it makes what I must do twice as hard. It is not easy to know you are sending some men to their deaths, even if they face death willingly, with love in their hearts."

I chose my words carefully, as if walking through thorns. "I cannot say 'I know,'" I said. "We both know that would be a lie. But I think, I hope—that an act done out of love has the power to wipe the slate clean, to absolve. You may not always wish to be a prince, but nothing, not even your own will, can change the fact that that is who you are.

"How much better, then, for you to send your soldiers into battle understanding their true value, acknowledging that their loss will be mourned. We may not have a choice but to fight, yet surely there is still a right way to send men into battle, and a wrong one."

Prince Jian took a step closer. He was so close I

could have reached out and touched him, though I did not.

"Who are you?" he asked in a strange, hoarse voice. "How can you say such things to me? How can one so young, a stranger I've just met, see so clearly the conflicts of my heart?"

My own heart was roaring in my ears, so loudly that it threatened to drown out any other sound.

Tell him, I thought. *Tell him that your heart understands his because his heart is like your own. Tell him you are as different as he is. Tell him his older brother is right. There is much more to you than meets the eye.*

I didn't, of course. Even as my heart urged my tongue to speak, my mind won the struggle. If I told this prince the truth, he would surely prove himself to be like all other men in one respect: He would judge what I could do on the basis of my sex. If he knew I was a girl, not only would he feel betrayed that I had deceived him, he would make me stay behind. And that was a risk I would not take. I had not come so far only to sit in my tent. I had come to help save China.

"I cannot answer that," I said, and thought I felt my own heart break a little at my response. "I am sorry."

"Don't be," said Prince Jian. "I think I know what you would say. I felt it yesterday as we stood side by side before the archery targets. Our hearts are joined; they are the same somehow. I don't pretend to understand it, but I believe it to be true."

"I do not claim to have the heart of a prince," I protested. Even in the darkness I caught the flash of his smile.

"No? Then maybe you've just proven my point, Little Archer. My brothers would tell you soon enough that my heart is not as royal as it should be."

"If they say that, then they are wrong," I answered confidently. "I believe you would do whatever it took to make China safe, even if it went against your own heart's desire. Surely that is what it means to be truly royal."

"Do you have no fear of what tomorrow may bring, then?" Prince Jian asked.

"Of course I do," I replied. "I have as much fear as any of your soldiers on this night, but my fear will not save China."

Prince Jian put a hand to his neck, to where the tunic that he wore parted to expose his throat. He made a motion I did not immediately comprehend. Then, as I watched, he lifted something from around his neck and extended it toward me. From his outstretched fingers hung a length of fine gold chain. At its end dangled a medallion.

"Take this," Prince Jian said.

"Highness," I protested, "I cannot. You do me too much honor."

"Take it," Prince Jian repeated. "Do not make me command you."

Slowly I reached for the chain, the tips of my fingers just barely brushing Prince Jian's. I held the medallion up so that it could catch the faint firelight. There was a raised symbol on the medallion's smooth, round surface.

"Can you see what is there?" asked Prince Jian.

I nodded. "It is a dragonfly."

"And what does the dragonfly symbolize?"

"Courage," I said.

"Courage," Prince Jian echoed. "Let me see you put it on."

I slipped the chain over my head, letting both chain and medallion slide down to hide beneath my tunic, just as the prince had worn it.

"That medallion was given to me many years ago," the prince said quietly. "When I was just a boy. It was a gift from Hua Wei, who was once my father's greatest general. He presented it to me when he returned me to my father, after rescuing me from the Huns.

"General Hua said that if ever I feared my courage might fail, I should remember our ancient symbol. I should remember the courage embodied by the strength of the fragile wings of the dragonfly."

"He sounds like a wise man," I said, battling with a fierce and sudden impulse to cry. I could almost hear my father speak the words, as if he stood beside me.

"My father's greatest general," Prince Jian had said.

"I believe he is a wise man," Prince Jian answered softly. "He helped me to remember that those who seem invincible are sometimes not so very strong. While those who seem small and fragile may carry great things inside them. Think of this tomorrow, Gong-shi, when you face the Huns."

"Sire, I will," I promised. And now I did kneel down, and Prince Jian did not stop me. "I have no gift of gold to give you in return, but I swear that I will give you all the courage in my heart. When that is spent, I will find the way to give you more."

"In that case," Prince Jian replied, "your gift is more valuable than gold. Whatever the future brings, I will always honor the strength of your heart. It reminds me to stay true to what I hold in mine.

"Now stand up, and don't think I didn't notice that you knelt down after all."

"Indeed it is true what they say," I said as I stood. "Prince Jian has keen eyes."

"And his archers are impudent," the prince replied. "And now I will say good night. Think of me when you face the Huns, and fight well, Little Archer."

"I will," I promised.

Without another word he turned and was gone.

Sixteen

Our company departed at daybreak, though we could not see the sun. Dark clouds lowered in the sky, and the wind had the raw sting to it that always meant snow. Li Po called the archers together; General Yuwen assembled the foot soldiers. Those of us on horseback would ride ahead, and half a day's swift march would bring us all to the second pass.

Once there we would await the Huns.

All three princes came to speed us on our way. Prince Guang's handsome face was impassive. If he was unhappy to have been overruled by his brothers, he did not show it in public.

"Take this," Prince Jian said, suddenly materializing at my side as I sat upon my horse awaiting orders. In his outstretched hands he held a war horn made of polished bone.

"This horn has been in my family for countless generations," the prince said. "It is said that its voice is that of China. Though the throats of a million enemies cry out for our blood, the voice of this horn will always be heard above them. If your need becomes dire and all else fails, sound the horn and I will come."

"My lord," I said, reaching down and taking the war horn. "I will do so."

The horn felt cool beneath my fingers. Its surface was elaborately carved; its mouthpiece, gold. As I tucked it beneath my shirt, I felt a moment of dizziness, as if I could feel the earth turning beneath my horse's feet as the prophecies about this prince began to come full circle.

Though, as Li Po gave the signal and our company began to move out, it seemed to me suddenly that the fate of China no longer lay in Prince Jian's hands or even in his heart. Now China's fate lay in mine.

We were cold and tired by the time we reached the small pass that was our destination, for the way was rocky and the riding hard. Though a fire and a hot meal would have been most welcome, we had neither. Even the best-tended fire will smoke a little, and we would risk nothing that might give away our location to the Huns.

After we had rested and eaten a cold meal, Li Po took a group of archers to reconnoiter the cliffs on the right side of the pass, while I led a second group to explore the left one. At the same time, Li Po sent scouts through the pass itself, that we might learn more of its terrain and determine if any additional information could be gathered about the whereabouts of the Huns.

"There is this much in our favor," Li Po said late that afternoon, after we had finished our reconnaissance. We were having our own small council session, just the two of us. The rest of the men were checking their equipment. The scouts had not yet returned, but we had posted a guard at the head of the pass. Our force might be small, but we would not be caught unawares.

"The cliffs are steep and rocky. They will provide us with good cover," Li Po continued.

"Now if only I knew whether to hope that Prince Jian is right about what the Hun leader intends, or that he is wrong," I replied.

"Try hoping that we are strong enough to meet whatever challenge comes our way," Li Po suggested.

"Captain!" I heard a voice call.

Quickly Li Po got to his feet. "Keep your voice down!"

"Apologies, Captain," the soldier, a man whose name I did not know, said in a quieter voice. "The scouts have returned. They have sighted the Huns."

"You are sure it was the Hun commander that you saw?" Li Po asked several moments later.

The scout leader stood bent over with his hands on his knees, breathing hard. The news he and his comrades carried back to camp was dire. A large Hun force was headed our way. It was commanded by the Hun leader himself.

"As sure as I can be," our scout leader said. He pulled in one more deep breath and then straightened up. "I saw their standard with my own eyes. A great horse, galloping."

"Perhaps it is a ruse," another scout suggested. "Meant to trick us."

"They have no need to do that," I said. "They believe the pass is unguarded."

"How large is their force?" Li Po asked. "Could you tell?"

"So large that we could not see them all," the scout leader replied. "We stayed as long as we dared, but we left before we could be seen, lest we give all of us away."

"You did well," Li Po answered at once. "You made the right choice. Go get some rest and what you can to eat. The rest of you, return to your posts. Gong-shi and I will confer about what to do next."

"We will never be able to hold them," Li Po said in a tense voice after the others had departed. "Even a small force would have tested our strength, but to face the Huns in such numbers . . ."

He eyed the war horn I wore slung around my neck. "Perhaps it is time to hear the voice of the war horn."

"No," I said decisively. "Not yet. That will only bring them on. They'll overwhelm us before we even have the chance to fight."

"You are up to something," Li Po said. "I can always tell. What is in your mind?"

"Give your fastest rider my father's horse," I said. "And have him ride for reinforcements. We have but two things in our favor: the narrowness of the pass and the element of surprise. Let us put them both to work for us."

"If only there were some way to block the pass completely," Li Po cried.

"I have been thinking about that," I said. "First send the messenger to Prince Jian. Then come with me. I have seen a place where we might attempt such a thing."

By the time the sun plunged behind the mountain, our plans were set. In addition to the man on horseback, Li Po had also sent his two swiftest runners to Prince Jian. No more horses could be spared, but it did not seem prudent to trust our information, or our fate, to just one man.

Shortly after sundown Li Po and I led the archers up into the cliffs. There, as silently as we could, we worked feverishly on the plan we hoped would ensure both our survival and China's.

Though the pass was never wide enough for more than two men to ride abreast, there was one spot where the passage grew so narrow that the legs of the riders seemed sure to brush against the sheer stone walls as the men rode side by side. This was the narrowest point of all, and it was here that Li Po and I hoped to create a rock slide. A rock slide big enough to block the passage so that no men could come through the gap afterward. Even if we didn't close the pass completely, we hoped to slow down the Hun army long enough for our own reinforcements to arrive.

It was exhausting work, cruel to the hands we

would need later to ply our bows. We labored through the night. At least the work took such concentration that none of us had much room to spare for thoughts about what would happen once the sun rose. We could only hope our plan would work and that word of the Huns' true intentions had reached the princes' camp.

We could only hope that some of us would survive.

Li Po called a halt several hours before daylight, sending the men back down the mountain for food and what sleep could be managed before dawn. After much discussion the two of us had decided that we must allow a great enough number of Hun soldiers to come through the pass to maintain the illusion that they remained undetected, that their plan was succeeding and they would catch the Chinese army by surprise. And here, at last, something about what the Huns were planning worked in our favor, for our scouts had reported that the Hun leader rode at the head of his column of soldiers.

Once we triggered the rock slide, the Hun leader would be cut off. He would be unable to turn back, and the main body of his forces would be rendered incapable of moving forward to join him. This would leave the Hun leader and his smaller group of soldiers with just one choice: to move forward, into China. There they would be confronted first with our force and then, if all went well, with reinforcements from the main Chinese army.

And the signal to trigger the avalanche, to set the whole plan in motion, would be one last warning to our own troops: the sounding of the war horn.

The first of the Hun soldiers entered the pass just as the sun rose in an angry, sullen sky. The wind had more bite to it than it had the day before. Now it was too cold to snow. I kept the fingers of my right hand, the one I would use to pull the bowstring, tucked into my armpit in an attempt to keep them warm. We could hear the Huns long before we could see them. The narrow gorge seemed to push the sound of the horses' hooves ahead of the animals themselves.

As had been the case for our reconnaissance the day before, I took my archers into the cliffs on the left of the pass while Li Po led his into the right. The pass was so narrow that I could actually see Li Po from where I crouched. I felt the dragonfly medallion the prince had given me, warm against my skin.

Courage, Mulan, I thought.

The sound of the Hun horses echoed against the stone walls, so loud that it seemed impossible that we could not see the horses and riders themselves. The sound seemed to rise to a fever pitch. As I watched from the far side of the pass, Li Po rose from his crouch. At this signal all our archers set the arrows to their bows, but they did not fire. Li Po held up one hand, palm facing outward.

Hold.

Now, finally, the first group of men and horses began to pass beneath us in a relentless, endless tide.

My arms and shoulders ached with the effort it took to hold the bow steady, and still Li Po did not give the order to fire. I saw the archer closest to me pull his lips back from his teeth in a grimace of determination and pain. Still, Li Po's hand never wavered.

Hold. Do not fire.

And then, suddenly, I saw it: a rider bearing a banner with the figure of a galloping horse, the standard of the Huns. Beside him rode a soldier with a great round shield. And just behind them was a single rider, alone. His horse was the most magnificent I had ever seen, his coat like burnished copper. The soldier's long, black hair was not tied back but streamed freely over his shoulders.

Surely this had to be the leader of the Huns.

Even from a distance it seemed to me that I could feel this man's restless energy, the determination that possessed him, propelling him forward. And I understood why others would follow such a man, even into these impossible conditions. There was something about his confidence and assurance that made the impossible seem possible.

I could feel my shoulders start to tremble with the strain of holding the bow taut. More than anything in the world I longed to let my arrow fly. Now the dragonfly medallion felt like a burning brand against my skin.

Lend me your strength and your determination, I thought. *Help me find the courage to hold on, to do what I must.*

The Hun leader and his standard-bearer were directly beneath us now. And finally, with one swift decisive motion, Li Po brought his hand down, giving the signal to fire. The air around me sang with the sound of bowstrings being released, the hiss of arrows as they sought their targets. The sound of men crying out in surprise and pain and the almost human screams of the horses rose up as if to surround us.

The Hun leader urged his troops forward, only to encounter the resistance of our own soldiers. The narrow pass seemed to roil like boiling water as men and horses jockeyed for position. Hun archers began to return our fire. The Hun standard-bearer lifted his face toward the cliffs as he screamed out his defiance. At that moment Li Po rose to his full height and sent an arrow straight toward him.

As the arrow hurtled downward, the standard-bearer sat hard in the saddle, trying to force his horse forward. But there was no room for him to maneuver. The way ahead was blocked by soldiers. Li Po's arrow pierced the banner and then buried itself deep into the standard-bearer's shoulder. Screaming in fury and pain, the bearer released the standard. It tumbled to the ground and was trampled by the feet of the horses.

Now the Hun leader rose in his stirrups, calling out to his soldiers in a great and terrible voice. He set an arrow to the string of his own bow, turned his horse to one side, and fired upward. I felt my heart leap into my throat. In his determination to see the

Hun standard fall, Li Po had forgotten to take cover. He was still standing, and because he was visible, he made the perfect target.

"Li Po!" I cried.

But even as I shouted, I knew it was too late. As if guided by an evil demon, the Hun leader's arrow found its mark. As Li Po toppled backward, I rose to my own feet and fired.

This was the shot that I had missed not three days before, through the neck, from side to side. As if he heard my cry of pain and despair over every other voice around him, the Hun leader swiveled his head in my direction.

My arrow caught him beneath the chin, piercing his throat clean through from one side to the other. With tears that threatened to blind my eyes, I dropped to my knees, letting go of my bow and reaching for the war horn. I put it to my lips, drew in a single breath, and sent forth its call. Into it I poured all the pain and courage that lay within my heart.

I made the war horn sing with the voice of China.

At once, the Chinese soldiers below me began to retreat down the pass, drawing a portion of the Hun troops after them. I waited as long as I dared, praying that as many of our men as possible were clear.

I put the horn to my lips and again made it bellow. This was the signal the archers had been waiting for. On both sides of the pass, they dropped their weapons and put their shoulders to the rocks we had labored so long and hard to loosen the night before. The very air seemed to quake and shudder as, with a great groan, the rocks gave way and the walls of the pass began to tumble downward toward the Hun soldiers below. A cloud of dust rose, thick and choking. For the third and final time, I blew into the war horn's mouth.

And then, without warning, the earth gave a great crack beneath my feet and I, too, was tumbling down. My last thought, before the world turned black, was that even if I would be crushed myself, at least I had helped to crush the enemies of China.

SEVENTEEN

I returned to myself slowly, as if trudging uphill through a long and narrow tunnel. It was dimly lit, yet not entirely dark, because it seemed to me that I saw faces of companions I had known and loved, passing in and out of focus as I walked.

I saw General Yuwen's face most often. Next came an ancient, wrinkled face I did not recognize. And every once in a while, when the tunnel seemed most steep and endless, when it seemed to me I could not take another step, I thought I saw the face of Prince Jian. He gazed down at me with an expression I could not read save for the sorrow in his eyes.

Once I thought I opened my eyes to see him sitting beside me, head bowed down, cradling in his hands the dragonfly medallion he had given me the night before the battle with the Huns. Another time I felt the medallion against my skin once more, but the tight hold of Prince Jian's hand on mine.

And finally there came a series of days when the tunnel proved too dark and steep to travel at all. It was then that I was seized by a great fire in all my limbs, when my ears grew deaf and my eyes grew blind. And in those days I could not even wonder whether my journey had, at last, reached its end. I could form no questions, for I was lost, even to myself.

When I opened my eyes at last, it was to light that was the color of a pearl, a color that I recognized, and I knew I had awakened just before dawn. For several moments I lay absolutely still, searching for some clue to my surroundings, staring upward as the light grew stronger. The answer came almost at once. I was in my own tent, the one I had once shared with Li Po. I was lying on the pallet that had once been my bed. My body felt . . . unfamiliar. Light as a seedpod spinning through the air, heavy as a stone, all at the same time.

I shifted, and felt pain shoot through my shoulder. *I have been injured*, I thought.

And at this the memories came flooding back. Memories of blood and pain, the screams of men and horses. I made a sound of protest, and in an instant Prince Jian was there, kneeling beside me. He took my hands in one of his and pressed his other hand against my brow.

"Your skin is cool to the touch," he said. "Praise all the gods, your fever has broken." His eyes roamed over me, his expression unreadable.

"I believe that you will live, Little Archer."

I tried to speak but managed only a croak because my mouth and throat were parched. As if he understood, Prince Jian released me, stepped away briefly, and then returned with a cup of cool water. He eased me upright, helping me to drink. I could take no more than a little, for in all my thirst I was weak and clumsy. Water dribbled down my chin and down onto my neck.

"Li Po," I managed to get out.

Prince Jian laid me back down. "Perhaps it would be better to wait . . . ," he began.

"No," I said. "No, tell me."

His eyes steady on mine, Prince Jian shook his head, and I knew the thing I feared had come to pass.

"I am sorry. I am told he died bravely," the prince said.

I nodded, blinking against the tears that filled my eyes. "He took down the standard. We were victorious?"

"Yes, we were victorious," Prince Jian replied. He fell silent, as if deciding what to say next.

He has grown older, I thought. There were lines around his mouth I didn't recognize, and his face looked pale and drawn. His shoulders, though still straight, now looked as though they carried some impossibly heavy burden.

"But the archers who fought beside you say that it was you who made our victory possible," the prince finally said. "They say you killed the Hun leader with a single shot. Is this so?"

"It is," I said, my voice a little stronger now. "But it was Li Po who made it possible. When the standard went down, the Hun leader turned his head toward me. It was . . ." I paused and took a breath. "It was the shot I missed that day when we practiced at targets."

"I see," Prince Jian said. "This bears out what I was told." His mouth twisted into a strange smile. "It would seem you are now a great hero, Little Archer."

He knows, I thought. *He knows that I'm a girl and not a boy.*

I had no idea how long I had been lying there, but I must have been tended by a physician. My true gender would have been discovered at once.

And now, for the first time, I felt my courage falter. I could not imagine how this prince, who had shared the innermost workings of his heart with me, could forgive the fact that I had kept something so important as my true identity from him.

"Highness," I said. "I—"

Prince Jian stood up. "I will bring General Yuwen to you," he said, speaking over my words. "He has been concerned about your welfare, spending many hours beside you. He will wish to know you are once more yourself."

At his choice of phrase I winced, for I had not truly been myself before. The difference was that now we both knew it.

He will never forgive me, I thought.

More than anything else in the world, I longed to call Prince Jian back, to explain all the reasons for what I had done. But I did not. I had betrayed his trust. And where there is no trust, it does no good to explain.

"Thank you," I said finally. "I would like to see General Yuwen to thank him for all his care."

"I will go, then," said Prince Jian. He moved to the tent flap, lifted a hand to push it back, and then paused.

"I am sorry for the loss of your friend," he said. Then he stepped through the opening and was gone.

General Yuwen came in several moments later. He strode at once to where I lay and knelt down beside me. Gently he took my hand in his.

"Mulan," he said simply. "My little hero of China."

At the sound of my true name the floodgates opened. I did not behave like a hero of China, brave at all costs. Instead I threw my good arm around General Yuwen as I would have liked to with my own father, burying my face in the crook of his neck, and I wept like a child for everything I had lost.

It was from General Yuwen that I learned the full story of the events of that day, and its aftermath. Now that my fever had broken, I began to make a speedy recovery. It was true that I was covered from head to feet in scrapes and cuts, in bruises that would have made Min Xian hiss like a steam kettle in sympathy. My right arm was in a sling. In my tumble down the mountain I had broken my collarbone. I had been so buried in rubble that it was a miracle I didn't have more broken bones. It was Prince Jian who had found me.

By the time I had made the war horn cry, a relief force had already been sent on its way to provide reinforcements. The messengers Li Po and I had sent had reached Prince Jian safely. The prince himself had led the relief force, an honor that, as the eldest, Prince Ying could have claimed as his own. But he had been gracious, acknowledging his youngest brother's wisdom in insisting that the second, smaller pass be protected—even over the objections of his brothers and their councilors.

"Never have I seen anyone fight as Prince Jian did that day," General Yuwen confided one night.

I was now well enough to be up for long periods of time. The general and I were sitting outside the tent before the bright blaze of a campfire. General Yuwen often came to spend his evenings with me, and he was not alone. Word that Gong-shi—the young archer whose shot had helped to save all China—was in fact a girl had spread quickly through the camp. Many of the soldiers came to pay their respects, but also, I suspected, to relieve their curiosity. Only Prince Jian stayed away. I had not seen him since the day I first awakened.

"The prince was like a tiger," General Yuwen continued now. "When the battle was over and we began to take stock of our wounded . . . When Li Po's body had been discovered but you could not be found . . ."

The general broke off, shaking his head. "Never have I seen anyone more determined," he went on. "One of the archers who had fought beside you was brought before him to explain what he thought had befallen you. It was long after nightfall. Prince Jian had had no rest and little food. Still he took a torch and went to search for you himself. He would not rest until he found you, he said."

"And after all that, I turned out to be a girl," I said quietly.

"Not just any girl," General Yuwen said. "Hua Wei's own daughter. Like your father before you, you are a hero, Mulan."

"You called me that before," I said. "But I don't feel very much like one, and I never set out to win that title."

"Perhaps that's why it fits you so well," the general answered quietly. "You thought not of yourself, of your own glory, but of China. The emperor is eager to meet you. He has even sent for your father."

Though winter was almost upon us, the emperor wished to celebrate China's great victory over her ancient enemy not in the capital but here, in the mountains where the battle had been fought. He was already on his way, with a great cavalcade of retainers. And my father was to be among them.

"So he is forgiven, then," I said.

"It would appear so," General Yuwen replied. "But, then, he was right after all. The Huns did present a danger, as long as the son of their former leader was alive. Now that he is dead, the Huns have no one to lead them. The next in line is an infant. It will be many years before he is grown.

"But the arrow that turned the tide in China's favor was fired by none other than Hua Wei's own child. It is your actions that have restored your father to favor."

"Even though I'm a girl?" I said.

General Yuwen smiled.

"And Prince Jian?" I asked. "Can I win back his favor by my actions, do you think?"

"Ah, Mulan," General Yuwen exhaled my name on a sigh. "There I think you must be patient. Give him time."

"I don't think there's enough of it," I said simply. "I hear what the men say around the fires at night. The Son of Heaven intends to make Prince Jian his heir, passing over Ying and Guang. A prince and a general's daughter might have found a way to bridge the gap between them, assuming I might be forgiven in the first place, but now . . ."

My voice trailed off. "Even if I am patient for the rest of my life, I think the gulf between us will be too great to cross."

General Yuwen remained silent. In spite of the warmth of the fire, I shivered, for I discovered that I was cold. And it seemed I might never be warm again, because this cold came not from the air around me but from the depths of my own heart.

I want to go home, I thought. I longed for the familiar branches of the plum tree, Min Xian's face. Most of all I longed for Li Po. But even when I returned, nothing would be quite the same. Li Po was gone, and the Mulan who would return was not a child anymore.

In the weeks since I had made the decision to leave my father's house, I had grown up. And I had learned that not every battle can be fought by firing an arrow from a bow. But I would have to face whatever new challenges came my way as bravely as I had faced the Huns. I could not wallow in self-pity, thinking about what might have been. I had to do my duty. It was the only way to stay true to myself.

I wonder if this is how Jian feels about the possibility of becoming emperor, I thought. Despite the rift between us, I believed I still understood what was in his heart, because it was just like mine. And what Prince Jian's heart wanted was to run free, to command no other than itself. But like my own heart would, Prince Jian's would accept his responsibilities. He would do his duty with his head held high. He would bring himself and his family honor.

I must learn to do the same, I thought.

I had to cease to mourn what could never be and learn to make the most of what was possible. And I would begin by trying to mend the hurts of the past.

Asking General Yuwen to bring me paper, brush, and ink, I sat up late, composing a letter of sympathy to Li Po's mother.

Eighteen

The very next morning the outriders appeared, giving us warning that the Son of Heaven would soon arrive. A great space had been prepared in the middle of the camp for his tent, with those of the princes flanking it on the left side, the side of the heart.

As soon as word reached him of his father's approach, Prince Ying sent soldiers to line the road-way, so many that they stood six deep. Not only would this give many men who had fought bravely the chance to see the emperor, it meant that the Son of Heaven would be welcomed by those who had fought for China's cause.

The minor court officials appeared first, followed by the members of the emperor's own household. The silk of their elaborate robes seemed to dazzle my eyes.

"There are so many of them," I murmured to General Yuwen.

He smiled. "That is not the half of them," he replied. "Only those most suited to travel. The rest stayed behind in Chang'an."

"No wonder my father found it quiet in the country," I said.

"Look!" General Yuwen said, pointing. "The Son of Heaven arrives!"

There was a flash of gold, like sunlight glancing off a mirror, and suddenly I could see the emperor himself. His horse was the color of sable. The Son of Heaven's cloak spread across the horse's back. Though lined with fur to protect him from the cold, it was also embellished with the figure of a five-clawed dragon embroidered in gold thread. The embroidery was so thick, the stitches so fine, that as the cloak shifted in the wind it seemed as if the dragon would leap from the emperor's back and take to the sky.

Straight to the center of camp the Son of Heaven rode, to where the princes stood in front of his tent to welcome him. As he approached, all those assembled knelt to do him honor. I had practiced kneeling and then standing up again, in the privacy of my tent. It's hard to kneel with only one arm for balance. The last thing I wanted was to humiliate myself and bring dishonor to my family by falling on my face as I paid homage to the Son of Heaven.

The emperor brought his horse to a halt.

"My sons, I come to celebrate your great victory," he said.

"Father," Prince Ying replied. "You are most welcome."

"I give thanks for your safety," the emperor went on, "as I give thanks for the safety of China. Rise now that you may look into my face and see how much I love and honor you."

At their father's instruction the princes stood, even as the emperor dismounted. He embraced each in turn.

"Where is the archer?" the emperor inquired. "Let me see Hua Wei's child."

I felt my heart give a great leap into my throat.

"There, Father," Prince Jian said. "Beside General Yuwen."

"Rise and come forward, child."

I did as the emperor commanded, a simple act that required every bit as much courage as facing down the Huns. Slowly I walked forward until I stood before the Son of Heaven.

"Tell me your name, Little Archer," he commanded, though his voice was not unkind.

"If it pleases Your Majesty," I said, astonished to hear my voice come out calm and steady. "I am Hua Mulan."

"I recognize your father's determination in your face," the emperor said.

"Majesty, you honor me to say so," I replied.

"Hear me now, all of you," the Son of Heaven cried in a great voice. "Once, long ago, in return for a great service I offered to grant Hua Wei the first wish of his heart. Now I offer this same gift to his daughter. For she has given me what I wished for most: the safety and security of China."

A great cheer went up from the soldiers. I stood, frozen in shock. The thought that the emperor might offer me such an honor had never even occurred.

What *was* the first wish of my heart?

Like my father, could I wish for love?

No, Mulan, I realized. *You cannot.* Not because I did not love, but because until this moment I had not recognized that love for what it truly was.

My father had spoken his wish, knowing he loved and was loved in return. But I was not so fortunate.

I cannot wish for love, I thought. *But I can wish because of it.* Prince Jian had given me the gift of courage when I had needed it most. Perhaps now I could give him something he would value just as much.

"Speak, Mulan," the Son of Heaven urged. "Tell me what I may grant you to show my gratitude."

"The Son of Heaven commands me to speak," I said, "and I will do so. This then is my reply: The first wish of my heart would be that you grant the first wish of a heart other than my own. A heart I will name, if you will let me.

"I have served China. I already have my reward."

There was a startled pause.

"Where is Hua Wei?" the emperor finally said. "Let him come forward."

"Here, if it pleases Your Highness," my father said.

"Your daughter speaks well, Hua Wei," the Son of Heaven complimented when my father had come to kneel before him.

"Your Highness honors us both to say so," my father replied.

The Son of Heaven frowned. "You are sure that is

your final answer?" he asked me. "You will give away your own wish to someone else? Who is this person whose heart you value so much?"

I took the deepest breath of my entire life. *Do it, Mulan*, I thought. *Show courage. Be true to yourself.*

Though the emperor had given me permission to stand, I knelt once more, at my father's side.

"I cannot answer that question, Majesty," I said.

"Why not?"

"Until I know that Your Majesty agrees to my request, I cannot speak the name aloud. For if I speak too soon, I throw away my wish."

At this, Prince Guang could contain himself no more.

"Father," his outraged voice rang out. "Surely this has gone on long enough. Much as I respect your wish to honor Hua Wei's daughter, I must—"

"What you must do"—the emperor's voice sliced through that of his son's—"is to show your respect by holding your tongue. I gave the girl leave to speak from her heart and she has done so. She displays great wisdom in also speaking her mind. I cannot ask for the first and then fault her for the second.

"Very well, Hua Mulan. You shall have what you desire. Name who you will, and he shall have the first wish of his heart. This I swear to you from my own. Now stand up and tell me who it is."

"The Son of Heaven is gracious and bountiful," I answered as I stood. "With all my heart I ask that you bestow your gift on Prince Jian. For it was he who first saw the way our enemies would try to defeat us. He is the true hero of China, not I."

"Jian, step forward," the emperor said.

"Father," Prince Jian said, even as he obeyed, "I cannot—"

"Why are all my sons suddenly so determined to tell me what I can and cannot do?" the Son of Heaven inquired. "Do you think that I am in my dotage? That I don't know my own mind?"

"Of course not, Father," Prince Jian protested.

"I am glad to hear it," the Son of Heaven answered. "Now do as I command." All of a sudden the emperor's tone softened. "Do not be afraid. No matter what it is, I will make the first wish of your heart the first desire of mine. I have sworn it. Therefore speak, my son."

"I will obey you in this, as in all things," Prince Jian said. I was grateful that he was standing next to me, for it meant I could not look at him. Instead I kept my eyes straight ahead, gazing at the emperor's elaborately embroidered cloak.

"This, then, is what I would ask of you, Father. Do not make me return to court. Instead let me stay in these wild lands. Let me dedicate my life to keeping China safe in her remotest places, for there I will be free to be myself."

"What you ask for is difficult to grant," the Son of Heaven said, his voice heavy. "For it runs counter to my hopes. But I have sworn to give you what you wish, and I will honor my word. So be it, Jian, my son.

You may serve China in the way that is closest to your heart.

"Come now." The emperor made a gesture, calling all his sons to his side. "Let us go inside and we will speak further of these things."

"Father," Prince Jian said, "I will do your bidding with all my heart."

As the Son of Heaven and his sons passed by me, I knelt once more. When he reached me, the emperor stopped.

"Hua Mulan."

"Yes, Mighty Emperor," I said.

"It seems I owe you a second round of thanks. You saw what was in my son's heart, while I saw only what was in my own. I will make sure to ask him how this might be so."

With that he strode past me and was gone. His sons followed in his wake. When they were safely inside the tent, I got to my feet and turned directly into my own father's waiting arms.

NINETEEN

"When I realized that you had gone, when I realized what you had done, I thought that I had lost you forever," my father told me later that night.

Though my father had feasted with the emperor, the princes, and the generals, he had left the celebrations early so that we might have some time alone. I had not gone to the celebration at all. Instead I had pleaded weariness and the pain of my wounds. General Yuwen had secured the emperor's permission for me to remain quietly in my tent. I did not think I would be missed, at least not by the Son of Heaven himself.

He had made good his promise. He would grant his best-loved son the first wish of his heart, but the emperor would not thank me for it. It robbed him of his own wish that Prince Jian succeed him. I wondered if his father might see the wisdom of Prince Jian's choice, in time.

There would be several days of celebration and ceremonies yet before the emperor's great army would disband and before my father and I would ride for home. Chances were good I would never see Prince

Jian again. I tried to tell myself that it was for the best. I didn't get very far.

"I am sorry I went away without saying good-bye." I brought my thoughts back to the present and my father. "But I could hardly tell you what I wanted to do. You would never have let me go."

"Of course I wouldn't," my father said. "What kind of father would I have been, then?"

I smiled. "The same kind you are now, I hope. One who loves his daughter well enough to forgive her." Without warning I felt the tears well up in my eyes. "Oh, *Baba*," I said. "I just want to see Zao Xing and Min Xian. I want to see the plum trees bloom in the spring. I want to go home."

"And so we shall, my Mulan. Zao Xing will be pleased to see you. I was afraid she'd worry herself sick the whole time you were away."

"How is the baby?" I asked.

"Growing strong. Zao Xing complains she will grow as great as a house before the baby arrives. Min Xian takes good care of them both."

"I'm glad to hear it," I said. "Keeping Zao Xing and the baby safe was part of the reason I went away in the first place. I could not bear . . . I did not wish . . ."

"My daughter," my father said as he gathered me close. "I know. I am so proud of you, and not just for your ability to sneak off with my horse or for your skills with a bow. I am proud of your generous heart. Someday I hope you will have the reward it longs for."

"I hope so too," I said.

"Mulan," my father went on, "there is something that I would like to tell you, a thing I should have spoken to you long before now."

I burrowed a little deeper in my father's arms. "I think I know what you want to say," I said. "You wish to tell me the name of my mother. Min Xian told me before I rode away. Please don't be angry with her. She said I should not ride without knowing."

"She was absolutely right," my father replied. "And I am not angry for it. Her heart was more generous than mine in this." My father kissed the top of my head, the first such affection I had ever known him to show.

"Come now," he went on. "Let's get you a good night's sleep."

"*Baba*," I said suddenly, "do we have to wait until the end of the week? Couldn't we go home tomorrow? I'm well enough to travel. Honestly I am."

"Let me see what Huaji has to say," said my father. "If you are well enough, and there is no other reason to stay, perhaps we may go. The emperor has already honored you. But if it is the Son of Heaven's pleasure, we must stay."

"I understand," I promised. "But you'll ask General Yuwen first thing tomorrow?"

"Why not ask me now?"

My father and I turned as General Yuwen made his way through the tent flap. He and my father greeted each other warmly. Then the general turned to me.

"Perhaps it is not my place to say this with your father sitting right beside you, but I have never been more proud of anyone than I was of you today, Mulan. You have saved China twice, I think. Once by taking a life. Today by giving Prince Jian the opportunity to ask for the life he truly desires.

"He will serve China, and himself, far better living the life of his heart than he would have in the life his father had chosen for him."

"And Prince Ying will become emperor someday?" I asked, remembering the general's belief that Prince Ying would be a fine emperor during peace.

General Yuwen nodded. "Now there is no reason for anything else to occur. This has been a good day for China."

"Then I have done my duty and am content," I said.

The general regarded me quietly for a moment. "I think," he finally said, "that you have one more duty to perform. Prince Jian has asked to speak with you. He is waiting nearby. He did not wish to intrude on you and your father."

"The prince wishes to speak with me?" I said, trying to ignore the way my heart quickened. "Why?"

"I think that must be for him to say," General Yuwen replied. "Shall I tell him to come?"

"No," I replied. "There is no need. I will go myself. Instead stay here with my father. I'm sure the two of you have many things to discuss. But if I feel my ears burning, I will know you talked of me, so be warned."

"We promise not to mention your name at all," my father said as he bundled me into a cloak. I didn't believe him for a moment.

And so I was smiling as I stepped out into the night. I stood for a moment, letting my eyes adjust. The tent had been bright with lantern light, but now a full moon hung in the clear night sky, wrapping everything around me in the embrace of its cool white glow. I had taken no more than half a dozen steps toward Prince Jian's tent when he materialized by my side.

"You came," Prince Jian said. "I wasn't sure you would."

"Of course I would," I answered, and now my heart was impossible to ignore. It beat painfully inside my chest for all the things that it desired, now out of reach.

Do not fool yourself, Mulan, I thought. *They were always out of reach.* I might as well have stretched out my arms to touch the moon in the sky.

"If only to say good-bye," I went on.

"Will you walk with me?" Prince Jian said. "The sky is bright tonight."

"Just so long as you watch out for any holes," I replied. "It will never do for me to fall and lose the use of both my arms."

In the moonlight I caught the flash of his smile. He stepped to my left side, and taking me lightly by my good arm, we began to walk together.

"That sounds more like you," Prince Jian said. "I

thought . . ." He paused, and then began again. "I thought I might have lost you."

My pride put up a brief struggle and then went down in flames. *Why shouldn't I tell the truth?* I wondered. *I'll never see him again after tonight.*

"No," I answered quietly. "You could never lose me. It simply isn't possible."

"Why?" Prince Jian suddenly burst out. "Why did you do it?"

I didn't even pretend to not know what he was talking about. Still, I paused. I wanted to choose my words with care, with more care than I had chosen any others in my life.

"When your father made his offer, I looked into my heart to see what it might wish for above all else," I replied. "But I discovered that, as powerful as he is, what I desired most lay beyond even the Son of Heaven's power to bestow.

"So I looked into my heart again, and I thought . . ." My voice choked off as, just for a moment, my nerve faltered.

Remember the dragonfly, Mulan, I thought.

"I thought—I hoped I saw the way to make things right between us," I said after a moment. "I never meant to deceive you."

I broke off again, and made a wry face.

"Or at least no more than I deceived everyone else by pretending to be a boy. That night, before I went away to fight, I wanted to speak, to tell you the truth, but I could not. I could not tell you who I really was.

"In spite of all the ways that you are unique, in this you would have been like everybody else. All you would have seen was that I was a girl. You would have made me stay behind."

"I think that you are right," Prince Jian said slowly. "But is this all?"

"I don't know what you mean," I said.

Prince Jian stopped walking, though he kept his hand on my arm. "Mulan. Today you gave me the chance to speak the truth of my heart. Will you not tell me the truth of yours? If the only reason you spoke to my father as you did was to settle a debt between us, it is more than paid. If that is all there is between us, then tell me so. I will go, and we will never speak of our hearts again, for we will never see each other.

"But before I let this happen, I ask you again: Is this all? Did your heart bestow its great gift for no other reason? Does it want nothing else from me?"

"I might ask you the same question," I replied, making a bold answer lest my heart read too much into his words and begin to hope too much. "You are a great prince. Why should you care what my heart wants?"

"The answer to that is simple enough," Prince Jian said. "Though discovering it was hard. It is because I love you."

How brave he is! I thought. For with that simple declaration, he had set all defenses aside and laid bare his heart. He had been unwilling to risk China, but it seemed that he would risk himself.

You must be no less brave, Mulan, I told myself.

"In that case, you are more powerful than the Son of Heaven," I said aloud. "You have done what he could not. You have given me the first wish of my heart."

"And what was that wish?" Prince Jian asked. "Please—I would like to hear you say it out loud."

"That you love me as I love you," I said. "But this was a gift that only you could bestow."

Jian turned me to him then, mindful of my injury, and took me in his arms. "Mulan," he murmured against my hair. "Mulan."

"I know my name," I murmured back.

I felt a bubble of laughter rise up within him, heard it burst forth before he could stop it.

"Yes, but I'm still getting used to it," he replied. "You must give me a little time yet."

"I will give you all the time I have," I vowed, and felt his arms tighten.

"What?" he asked, his voice light and teasing even as he held me close. "No more?"

"Even this great hero of China has her limits, Majesty," I answered.

He tilted my face up and looked down into my eyes. "No," he said softly. "I really don't think so. That is one of the reasons I love you so much."

I reached up and laid a palm against his cheek.

"You have to stop this," I replied. "You'll make my head swell as well as make it spin."

As our lips met, we were both smiling. Our first kiss was full of the promise of both our hearts. A kiss of true love.

"I cannot promise you an easy life," the prince said when at last we broke apart. "But I hope that you will choose to share it with me anyway."

"Tell me something, Your Highness," I said. "Does anything about me tell you that I want an easy life?"

He laughed then, the cold night air ringing with the sound.

"No," he answered honestly. "Nothing does. Will you marry me, Mulan? Will you make your life with me in China's wild places, where our hearts may run as free as they desire?"

"I will," I promised. "But first I must return to my father's house. My stepmother is going to have a child. I would like to be there when it arrives."

"I will come with you," Prince Jian said. "I would like to meet Li Po's family."

"I love you," I said as the tears filled my eyes. "I love you with all my heart."

"I am glad to hear it," Prince Jian answered. "For I love you with all of mine. Though I suppose I should have asked your father's permission first."

"I believe that he will give it," I said. "For if there is one thing my father understands, it's marrying for love."

We were married in the spring, beneath the plum tree. Its blossoms were just beginning to fade and loosen their hold. Each time the wind moved through the branches, fragrant petals showered down around us. Neither the emperor nor either of Jian's brothers came to the ceremony. But General Yuwen was there, and Zao Xing, holding my baby brother in her arms. He had made his appearance early, causing us all alarm. But he soon proved the rightness of his choice, for he was growing fat and strong. In honor of my recent exploits, and to encourage him to grow up big and strong, my parents named him *Gao Shan*, High Mountain.

The night before Jian and I exchanged our vows, I could not sleep. I lay awake for many hours gazing out the window at the stars. I heard a soft whisper of sound and turned from the window to discover that my stepmother had entered my room, my baby brother in her arms.

"I wondered if I would find you awake," she said. "I don't think I slept a wink the night before I married your father."

"My own marriage will be all right, then," I said as I patted the bed beside me. "Look how well yours turned out."

Zao Xing chuckled as she sat. I held out my arms for the baby, and she placed Gao Shan into my arms.

"I won't be here to watch him grow up after all," I said.

"No," my stepmother said softly. "It appears that you will not. But I hope you won't stay away forever. Who knows? Perhaps you will return to have your own child."

"For goodness' sake, I'm not even married yet," I

exclaimed. Zao Xing clapped a hand over her mouth to keep from laughing as the baby squirmed in my arms.

"Here, take him back," I said. "I want to give him something."

Zao Xing took the baby back. He settled peacefully in the crook of her arm. I reached around my neck and lifted the dragonfly medallion over my head. I held it out in one palm.

"Prince Jian gave me this," I said, "the night before I rode away to fight the Huns. He said my father had given it to him when he was just a boy. I would like Gao Shan to have it, to remind him of Jian and me when we are far from home."

"It's a wonderful gift," Zao Xing said, her eyes shining. "Thank you, Mulan. He is too young to wear it yet, I think, but I will save it for him. And I will tell him of his famous sister's exploits. They will make fine bedtime stories."

"I'm not so sure that's a good idea," I said. "He'll grow up getting into trouble."

"No," Zao Xing replied. "He will grow up to bring the Hua family honor." She leaned over and kissed me on the cheek. "Your father and I are both glad to see you so happy, but we will miss you, Mulan."

"I'll miss you, too," I said. I returned her embrace.

"Now," Zao Xing said. "You lie back down. Gao Shan seems happy. I think we'll just sit beside you awhile."

The last thing I saw before I closed my eyes was

my stepmother cradling my baby brother in her arms. I fell asleep to the sound of her gentle voice singing a lullaby.

My father gave me his horse as a wedding gift.

"Ride up the streambed," he said when at last the day arrived for Jian and me to depart. "It will take you through the woods to where our land ends and the rest of China begins, and you will understand why I chose that path to return home."

"We will do so," I promised. I swung up into the saddle. "Make sure you teach my little brother how to use a bow."

"Come back and teach him yourself," my father said.

"I will do that also," I answered with a smile.

"Take good care of my daughter," my father said to Jian.

"As you once cared for me," he vowed. Then he grinned. "Though, truly, I think you may have things backward."

The sound of laughter filled our ears at our departure. Jian and I rode up the streambed as my father had requested, the horses picking their way carefully among the stones.

"I wonder why your father wanted us to go this way," Jian mused as we rode along.

"I can't say for certain," I said. "Though I think I'm beginning to guess. Wait until we reach the woods. Then we will know."

Half an hour's travel farther brought us to the first of the trees. Soon we had passed beneath their boughs.

"Look," I said, pointing. "Oh, look, Jian."

Here and there on the forest floor, now hidden, now revealing themselves, tiny white blossoms lifted up their heads.

Wild orchids.

DON'T MISS THIS MAGICAL TITLE
IN THE ONCE UPON A TIME SERIES!

BELLE
A Retelling of "Beauty and the Beast"

BY CAMERON DOKEY

Celeste. April. Belle.

Everything about my sisters and me was arranged in this fashion, in fact. It was the way our beds were lined up in our bedroom; our places at the dining table, where we all sat in a row along one side. It was the order in which we got dressed each morning and had our hair brushed for one hundred and one strokes each night. The order in which we entered a room or left it, and were introduced to guests. The only exception was when we were allowed to open our presents all together, in a great frenzy of paper and ribbons, on Christmas morning.

This may seem very odd to you, and you may wonder why it didn't to any of us. All that I can say is that order in general, but most especially the order in which one was born, was considered very important in the place where I grew up. The oldest son inherited his father's house and lands. Younger daughters did not marry unless the oldest had first walked down the aisle. So if our household paid strict attention to which sister came first, second, and (at long last) third, the truth is that none of us thought anything about the arrangement at all.

Until the day Monsieur LeGrand came to call.

Monsieur LeGrand was my father's oldest and closest friend, though Papa had seen him only once and that when he was five years old. In his own youth, Monsieur LeGrand had been the boyhood friend of Papa's father, Grand-père Georges. It was Monsieur LeGrand who had brought to Grand-mère Annabelle the sad news that her young husband had been snatched off the deck of his ship by a wave that curled around him like a giant fist, then picked him up and carried him down to the bottom of the ocean.

In some other story, Monsieur LeGrand might have stuck around, consoled the young widow in her grief, then married her after a suitable period of time. But that story is not this one. Instead, soon after reporting his sad news, Monsieur LeGrand returned to the sea, determined to put as much water as he could between himself and his boyhood home.

Eventually, Monsieur LeGrand became a merchant specializing in silk, and settled in a land where silkworms flourished, a place so removed from where he'd started out that if you marked each city with a finger on a globe, you'd need both hands. Yet even from this great distance, Monsieur LeGrand did not forget his childhood friend's young son.

When Papa was old enough, Grand-mère Annabelle took him by the hand and marched him down to the waterfront offices of the LeGrand Shipping Company. For, though he no longer lived in the place where he'd grown up, Monsieur LeGrand maintained a presence in our seaport town. My father then began the process that took him from being the boy who swept the floors and filled the coal scuttles to the man who knew as much about the safe passage of sailors and cargo as anyone.

When that day arrived, Monsieur LeGrand made Papa his partner, and the sign above the waterfront office door was changed to read LEGRAND, DELAURIER AND COMPANY. But nothing Papa ever did, not marrying Maman nor helping to bring three lovely daughters into the world, could entice Monsieur LeGrand back to where he'd started.

Over the years, he had become something of a legend in our house. The tales my sisters and I spun of his adventures were as good as any bedtime stories our nursemaids ever told. We pestered our father with endless questions to which he had no answers. All that he remembered was that Monsieur LeGrand had been straight and tall. This was not very satisfying, as I'm sure you can imagine, for any grown-up might have looked that way to a five-year-old.

Then one day—on my tenth birthday, to be precise—a letter arrived. A letter that caused my father to return home from the office in the middle of the day, a thing he never does. I was the first to spot Papa, for I had been careful to position myself near the biggest of our living room windows, the better to watch for any presents that might arrive.

At first, the sight of Papa alarmed me. His face was flushed, as if he'd run all the way from the waterfront. He burst through the door, calling for my mother, then dashed into the living room and caught me up in his arms. He twirled me in so great a circle that my legs flew out straight and nearly knocked Maman's favorite vase to the floor.

He'd had a letter, Papa explained when my feet were firmly on the ground. One that was better than any birthday present he could have planned. It came from far away, from the land where the silkworms flourished, and it informed us all that, at long last, Monsieur LeGrand was coming home.

Not surprisingly, this threw our household into an uproar. For it went without saying that ours would be the first house Monsieur LeGrand would come to visit. It also went without saying that everything needed to be perfect for his arrival.

The work began as soon as my birthday celebrations were complete. Maman hired a small army of extra servants, as those who usually cared for our house were not great enough in number. They swept the floors, then polished them until they gleamed like gems. They hauled the carpets out of doors and beat them. Every single picture in the house was taken down from its place on the walls and inspected for even the most minute particle of dust. While all this was going on, the walls themselves were given a new coat of whitewash.

But the house wasn't the only thing that got polished. The inhabitants got a new shine as well. Maman was all for us being reoutfitted from head to foot, but here, Papa put his foot down. We must not be extravagant, he said. It would give the wrong impression to Monsieur LeGrand. Instead, we must provide his mentor and our benefactor with a warm welcome that also showed good sense, by which my father meant a sense of proportion.

So, in the end, it was only Papa and Maman who had new outfits from head to foot. My sisters and I each received one new garment. Celeste, being the oldest, had a new dress. April had a new silk shawl. As for me, I was the proud owner of a new pair of shoes.

It was the shoes that started all the trouble, you could say. Or, to be more precise, the buckles.

They were made of silver, polished as bright as mirrors. They were gorgeous and I loved them. Unfortunately, the buckles caused the shoes to pinch my feet, which in turn made taking anything more than a few steps absolute torture. Maman had tried to warn me in the shoe shop that this would be the case, but I had refused to listen and insisted the shoes be purchased anyhow.

"She should never have let you have your own way in the first place," Celeste pronounced on the morning we expected Monsieur LeGrand.

My sisters and I were in our bedroom, watching and listening for the carriage that would herald Monsieur LeGrand's arrival. Celeste was standing beside her dressing table, unwilling to sit lest she wrinkle her new dress. April was kneeling on a cushion near the window, the silk shawl draped around her shoulders, her own skirts carefully spread out around her. I was the only one actually sitting down. Given the choice between the possibility of wrinkles or the guarantee of sore feet, I had decided to take my chances with the wrinkles.

But though I was seated, I was hardly sitting still. Instead, I turned my favorite birthday present and gift from Papa—a small knife for wood carving that was cunningly crafted so that the blade folded into the handle—over and over between my hands, as if the action might help to calm me.

Maman disapproves of my wood carving. She says it isn't ladylike and is dangerous. I have pointed out that I'm just as likely to stab myself with an embroidery needle as I am to cut myself with a wood knife. My mother remains unconvinced, but Papa is delighted that I inherited his talent for woodwork.

"And put that knife away," Celeste went on. "Do you mean to frighten Monsieur LeGrand?"

"Celeste," April said, without taking her eyes from the street scene below. "Not today. Stop it."

Thinking back on it now, I see that Celeste was feeling just as nervous and excited as I was. But Celeste almost never handles things the way I do, or April either, for that matter. She always goes at things head-on. I think it's because she's always first. It gives her a different view of the world, a different set of boundaries.

"Stop what?" Celeste asked now, opening her eyes innocently wide. "I'm just saying Maman hates Belle's knives, that's all. If she shows up with one today, Maman will have an absolute fit."

"I know better than to take my wood-carving knife into the parlor to meet a guest," I said as I set it down beside me on my dressing table.

"Well, yes, you may *know* better, but you don't

always *think*, do you?" Celeste came right back. She swayed a little, making her new skirts whisper to the petticoats beneath as they moved from side to side. Celeste's new dress was a pale blue, almost an exact match for her eyes. She'd wanted it every bit as much as I'd wanted my new shoes.

"For instance, if you'd thought about how your feet might *feel* instead of how they'd *look*, you'd have saved yourself a lot of pain, and us the trouble of listening to you whine."

I opened my mouth to deny it, then changed my mind. Instead, I gave Celeste my very best smile. One that showed as many of my even, white teeth as I could. I have very nice teeth. Even Maman says so.

I gave the bed beside me a pat. "If you're so unconcerned about the way you look," I said sweetly, "why don't you come over here and sit down?"

Celeste's cheeks flushed. "Maybe I don't want to," she answered.

"And maybe you're a phony," I replied. "You care just as much about how you look as I do, Celeste. It just doesn't suit you to admit it, that's all."

"If you're calling me a liar—," Celeste began hotly.

"Be quiet!" April interrupted. "I think the carriage is arriving!"

Quick as lightning, Celeste darted to the window, her skirts billowing out behind her. I got to my feet, doing my best to ignore how much they hurt, and followed. Sure enough, in the street below, the grandest carriage I had ever seen was pulling up before our door.

"Oh, I can't see his face!" Celeste cried in frustration as we saw a gentleman alight. A moment later, the peal of the front doorbell echoed throughout the house. April got to her feet, smoothing out her skirts as she did so. In the pit of my stomach, I felt a group of butterflies suddenly take flight.

I really did care about the way I looked, if for no other reason than how I looked and behaved would reflect upon Papa and Maman. All of us wanted to make a good impression on Monsieur LeGrand.

"My dress isn't too wrinkled, is it?" I asked anxiously, and felt the butterflies settle down a little when it was Celeste who answered.

"You look just fine."

"The young ladies' presence is requested in the parlor," our housekeeper, Marie Louise, announced from the bedroom door. Marie Louise's back is always as straight as a ruler, and her skirts are impeccably starched. She cast a critical eye over the three of us, then gave a satisfied nod.

"What does Monsieur LeGrand look like, Marie Louise?" I asked. "Did you see him? Tell us!"

Marie Louise gave a sniff to show she disapproved of such questions, though her eyes were not unkind.

"Of course I saw him," she answered, "for who was it who answered the door? But I don't have time to stand around gossiping any more than you have time to stand around and listen. Get along with you, now. Your parents and Monsieur LeGrand are waiting for you in the parlor."

With a rustle of skirts, she left.

My sisters and I looked at one another for a moment, as if catching our collective breath.

"Come on," Celeste said. And, just like that, she was off. April followed hard on her heels.

"Celeste," I begged, my feet screaming in agony as I tried to keep up. "Don't go so fast. Slow down."

But I was talking to the open air, for my sisters were already gone. By the time I made it to the bedroom door, they were at the top of the stairs. And by the time I made it to the top of the stairs, they were at the bottom. Celeste streaked across the entryway, then paused before the parlor door, just long enough to give her curls a brisk shake and clasp her hands in front of her as was proper. Then, without a backward glance, she marched straight into the parlor with April trailing along behind her.

Slowly, I descended the stairs, then came to a miserable stop in the downstairs hall.

Should I go forward, I wondered, *or should I stay right where I am?*

No matter who got taken to task over our entry later—and someone most certainly would be—there could be no denying that I was the one who would look bad at present. I was the one who was late. I'd probably already embarrassed my parents and insulted our honored guest. *Perhaps I should simply slink away, back to my room*, I thought. I could claim I'd suddenly become ill between the top of the stairs and the bottom, that it was in everyone's best interest that I hadn't made an appearance, particularly Monsieur LeGrand's.

And perhaps I could flap my arms and fly to the moon.

That's when I heard the voices drifting out of the parlor.

There was Maman's, high and piping like a flute. Papa's with its quiet ebb and flow that always reminds me of the sea. Celeste and April I could not hear at all, of course. They were children and would not speak unless spoken to first. And then I heard a voice like the great rumble of distant thunder say:

"But where is la petite Belle?"

And, just as real thunder will sometimes inspire my feet to carry me from my own room into my parents', so too the sound of what could be no other than Monsieur LeGrand's voice carried me through the parlor door and into the room beyond. As if to make up for how slowly my feet had moved before, I overshot my usual place in line. Instead of ending up at the end of the row, next to April, I came to a halt between my two sisters. April was to my left and Celeste to my right. We were out of order for the first and only time in our lives.

I faltered, appalled. For I was more than simply out of place; I was also directly in front of Monsieur LeGrand.

About the Author

CAMERON DOKEY

is the author of nearly thirty young adult novels. Her other titles in the Once upon a Time series include *Belle*, *Sunlight and Shadow*, *Before Midnight*, *Golden*, *Beauty Sleep*, and *The Storyteller's Daughter*. Her other Simon & Schuster endeavors include a book in the Simon Pulse Romantic Comedies line, *How NOT to Spend Your Senior Year*. Cameron lives in Seattle, Washington.

Need a distraction?

Julie Linker

Amy Belasen & Jacob Osborn

Anita Liberty

Lauren Baratz-Logsted

Teri Brown

Eileen Cook

From Simon Pulse
Published by Simon & Schuster

I look out the window,
and although it's dark,
the moon
illuminates the scene
as if a faraway
floodlight
is hung
from the sky.

So much whiteness.
Everywhere.

Come back,
angel.

Let us fly
away
from
here.

Also by Lisa Schroeder

From Simon Pulse | Published by Simon & Schuster

A promise broken. A secret betrayed.
What do you believe?

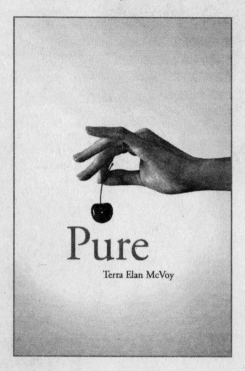

Pure

Terra Elan McVoy

"I love this book."
—Lauren Myracle, bestselling author of *ttyl* and *ttfn*

From Simon Pulse
Published by Simon & Schuster